Sir Galahad,
Mr. Longfellow,
and Me

Sir Galahad, Mr. Longfellow, and Me

BETTY HORVATH

A JEAN KARL BOOK

Atheneum Books for Young Readers

Atheneum Books for Young Readers
An imprint of Simon & Schuster Children's Publishing Division
1230 Avenue of the Americas
New York, New York 10020

Book design by Nina Barnett.
The text of this book is set in Bodoni.

First Edition
Printed in the United States of America
10 9 8 7 6 5 4 3 2 1

Library of Congress Cataloging-in-Publication Data
Horvath, Betty F.
Sir Galahad, Mr. Longfellow, and me / Betty Horvath.—1st ed.
p. cm.
"A Jean Karl Book."
Summary: In 1938, encouraged by her sixth-grade teacher, Emily
taps an unsuspected talent for writing poetry and makes many dis-
coveries about friends, family, and life.
ISBN 0-689-81470-4
[1. Schools—Fiction. 2. Poets—Fiction. 3. Family life—Fiction.]
I. Title
PZ7.H7922Si   1998
[Fic]—dc20
96-43460

In the order of their appearance:
Emily Keller, Maggie Horvath, Rebecca
Keller, and Sam Horvath

Chapter One

MAYBE THERE IS SOMEPLACE that's hotter than Missouri in the summer. Maybe. The equator. The inside of a volcano. H-e-l-l, if the preachers are right.

That's one reason why I'm usually glad to see the end of summer. It will get cooler. The other reason is that school will start.

Okay, I like school. Every year about the middle of August I start getting excited just thinking about all the new things, like bigger books, clean, unused tablets, long, sharp pencils, new dresses (mine made by Mama on her Singer sewing machine. I wish they came from Sears, Roebuck or Penney's like everybody else's), new socks, maybe new shoes.

I think about recess and my gang of girls that gather on the far side of the school yard under the tree that "belongs" to us. But this summer, in the Year of Our Lord 1938 (I won-

1

der why they say that?), I have mixed feelings. It's been a better-than-usual summer, and I'm not sure I'm ready to trade it in on school yet.

It's been too hot, as usual. The ice card has been up in the front window nearly every day for the iceman to leave twenty-five pounds of ice for the icebox on the back porch. Nights are too hot to sleep in the stuffy, airless bedroom I share with Marjy and Edith, so I take a couple of quilts and make a pallet on the screened back porch. I listen to the tree frogs and the faint buzz saw of a mosquito and try to count the stars. I watch the moon slowly cross the sky, so bright you could almost read by it. Long tree shadows creep across the yard.

There's something hurtful and sad about these still summer nights. Just listen to that whippoorwill. That's the lonesomest sound I know of, except maybe a train whistle or a French harp. I listen to the whippoorwill and I think about all the years ahead of me and I wonder about them. My head tells me that I won't always be spending my summer nights sleeping here on this back porch in a small town in Missouri, with Daddy and Mama inside, with Marjy and Edith in the room we share, and with Buddy and Joe-Joe asleep and quiet for a change.

So where *will* I be? What will I do when

I'm not eleven years old and living in this crowded little house with my family?

There are two pictures I get in my head when I ask myself that question. In the first picture I am poor, hungry, homeless, and all alone. In the other picture, I'm a glamorous, successful, interesting young woman with a wonderful job of some kind. I don't seem to be working very hard at it, though, because I'm driving a shiny yellow car north somewhere, along a seacoast. The car is a roadster, with the top down, and my dark hair (dark hair? When did I get dark hair?) is flying in the wind and I'm singing, on my way to someplace exciting and maybe romantic.

Romantic. That's the main reason I'm not as eager as usual for the summer to end. This has been a romantic summer. Not for me, of course, except as an interested spectator. But with two older sisters and three older cousins, I've had a kind of beginner's course in Romance this summer as I watched what my older relatives were up to, particularly my cousin Jean, who is sixteen going on twenty, according to Aunt Katy.

Marjy, Edith, and I have three cousins about our ages, who live in Springfield, which is about 150 miles away as the crow flies. We see them once or twice a year for a few days, either at their house or ours, and it's a loud, happy time with picnic-style meals and singing and laughing and staying up late and people sleeping all over the house.

The grown-ups have a good time too, especially Daddy and Uncle Sam who sit on the front porch with their feet propped up on the railing and tell and retell old family stories that all us kids, sitting on the steps, can repeat, word for word, right along with them. Uncle Sam gives Daddy a cigar, and Daddy accepts it doubtfully, with "I gave up smoking twenty years ago," then lights it up and puffs away contentedly.

Mama and Aunt Katy are busy competing in the kitchen. Aunt Katy puts together her famous bean salad and makes approving noises as she tastes it. Mama takes a couple of perfect lemon meringue pies out of the oven, and doesn't say anything but is careful to set them in an eye-catching spot where they are sure to be admired.

After supper we all gravitate to the piano where Daddy, who hasn't raised his voice in song for the past year, is persuaded to sing his specialty, "I'll Take You Home Again, Kathleen," in his fine tenor voice, with Uncle Sam rumbling a wordless bass note here and there.

Our Springfield cousins are a source of envy to us a lot of the time. It seems to us that they get to do a lot of things that we aren't allowed to do. Like wear snow pants when it's cold. According to Daddy, that isn't ladylike. Our ladylike legs can be blue with cold in our ladylike cotton stockings under our ladylike dresses, and the most sympathy we would get from Daddy would be an invitation to back up against the coal heat stove to thaw out.

Uncle Sam laughs a lot too, a family trait that has somehow skipped Daddy. We often compare Daddy and Uncle Sam for desirable fatherlike qualities and, to tell the truth, Daddy doesn't always come out ahead.

On the other hand, there is Aunt Katy who can't compare with Mama in any department, being sharp-tongued and short-tempered and very quick to swat first and ask questions later.

"Better look out or I'll smack you one!" she says, with her hand already making contact with the daughter she's "warning."

Mama isn't like that at all. She's soft-spoken, gentle, and not given to beating up on small children. So while our cousins may seem to live a more adventuresome life, having a car and always going on picnics and to parks and on Sunday afternoon drives, we usually feel the scales are pretty evenly balanced, with Mama being the asset she is.

Anyhow, it has been an interesting summer and it hasn't seemed as long as usual because Marjy, Edith, and I spent two weeks of it in Springfield with our cousins Jean, Diana, and Catherine. We took the train. All by ourselves, if you don't count the everlasting ghostlike presence of Daddy whose advice and instructions covering every possible emergency resounded in our ears in a most lifelike way: "Don't talk to strangers. When you change trains in Carthage, don't leave the station. (Never mind that it was a three-hour layover.) Watch your pocketbooks. Remember you are *Campbells!*"

Somewhat to our surprise, considering all the dire warnings, it was an uneventful (though heady-with-freedom) trip, and we settled down to two weeks of unaccustomed independence.

Maybe Aunt Katy is made of better stuff than I've been giving her credit for, to willingly agree to having six girls between the ages of eleven and sixteen in her care for two whole weeks.

Of course, we weren't around the house and underfoot much of the time. We roamed in a gang all over Springfield, either on foot or in Jean's boyfriend's car, which he drove at terrifying speeds, with one careless hand on the steering wheel and his other arm around Jean.

That's what I mean about the romantic summer. It was Jean and Carl who were giving romantic lessons. Springfield is a kind of big country town. Halfway down the block from Aunt Katy and Uncle Sam's house there is a large garden with a big cornfield, and whenever we couldn't find Jean, you could bet that she and Carl were standing out in the middle of that cornfield, hidden in the forest of tall green stalks, just standing there glued together and kissing like mad.

Of course, we didn't tell Aunt Katy and Uncle Sam about the wild car rides, and we didn't tell them about all the kissing going on. To tell the truth, I didn't care much for those car rides. They were scary. But I was interested in this kissing stuff. It was hard to figure. I mean, I can understand kissing somebody you like once in a while, but why in the world would you want to stand out in a hot, dusty cornfield, being tickled by prickly dry cornstalk leaves, with the sun beating down on you and sweat pouring off you, glued to another hot body with your mouth pasted on his for a long, long time? Jean says I'll understand it when I'm sixteen. I wonder.

When Jean wasn't out in the cornfield kissing Carl, she was seated at the piano, her long fingers rippling out love song after love song, or she was floating around the house with a dreamy look on her face and singing the song we always heard Kenny Baker sing on *Your Hit Parade* on Saturday night, something about how "love walked right in and drove the shadows away."

So, it had been a romantic summer. I was sorry when the two weeks were over and it was time to leave Springfield. I'm not likely to be that close to romance again in a long time. And it certainly isn't going to happen to *me*!

Well, it's late August now, August 24, 1938, to be exact, and school will be starting soon. So far, that's always been better than just about anything else, and that probably includes Romance. I expect it will be this year too.

Chapter Two

THIS IS MY SEVENTH YEAR at Park School, if you count kindergarten. Sixth grade is as far as you can go. After that, it's the junior high school across town. So, this being my last year at Park, I want it to be special. I want to leave my mark on it. "Footprints on the sands of time," as Henry Wadsworth Longfellow puts it.

Maybe some day they'll put a brass plaque above the blackboard that says "Emily Ann Campbell Studied Here." Sort of like those signs all over New England that claim "George Washington Slept Here." But I'll have to get famous first.

It could happen. Look at it this way: Every famous person you ever heard of was eleven years old once. And they weren't famous then. So I figure my chances right now are about as good as any other eleven-year-old. Maybe better than some. Better than Norman Olsen who's always trying to copy my spelling test. Although, he *is* the school marbles tournament champion, so I guess I have to allow that he might get famous for something more or less athletic like that. But that's not the kind of famous I'm talking about.

I'm talking about Achievement Famous. Or Noble Famous. Or Artistically Famous. The problem is, I'm not sure what I'm going to do that's going to make the world, and especially Park School, sit up and take notice.

We can probably forget about Noble Famous. I have to be honest. I'm sorry, but I just don't want to go off to some poor, backward country and live in dirt and get bitten and stung by strange and dangerous bugs and animals and be uncomfortable all the time. I admire Dr. Albert Schweitzer, but I don't want to *be* Dr. Albert Schweitzer. Nor Florence Nightingale. When I was little, I used to think it would be grand and glorious to be a nurse and heal the sick and wounded, but it turns out that I don't like blood and messy body stuff, so being an angel of mercy is out.

It would be exciting to be an explorer and discover new things, but by the time I grow up there probably won't be anything left on earth to discover. Anyhow, I think with exploring, you have to consider the discomfort factor, things like your chances for being too cold, too hot, hungry, thirsty. Lost. Dead. And we already know I don't like that kind of thing.

Movie star? Nope. Not pretty enough. Not that I'm ugly, mind you, but I don't have curly hair or red Cupid's-bow lips or a slinky walk.

I might be a poet. With all respect to Mr. Longfellow, I think I could come up with something as good or better than:

Listen, my children, and you shall hear,
Of the midnight ride of Paul Revere.

Of course, I don't say this to my teachers who, so far, all seem to think this is a pretty good poem. I wonder if they've ever read "The Highwayman" or "The High Tide on the Coast of Lincolnshire" or "Sir Galahad"? That's the kind of poetry *I* plan to write if I decide to become a poet.

I know all of those, and lots more, by heart and sometimes I say them to myself when I'm walking. I can't help it. The rhythm gets into my feet and before I know it, I'm walking along in iambic pentameter (look it up). Annoying after a while, but useful in the winter. It takes my mind off how cold my lady-like legs are in their ladylike cotton stockings under my ladylike dress. I suppose *Paul Revere's Ride* would work for that too, but I haven't bothered to memorize it.

All this was going through my mind as I tied the laces on my (new!) shoes a final time and gave a last-minute check to myself in the mirror. I was wearing a new dress that Mama had made (sigh), white with blue windowpane checks. It had a square neck and a fitted bodice that came down to a point in front, and a skirt that flared out in all directions. Actually, it looked pretty good. Almost as good as a Montgomery Ward dress. Not a bad way to start off to school on the first day. I might even pass Ruby Weber's critical inspection.

Ruby Weber has a whole closetful of Montgomery Ward dresses. She will be glad to tell you exactly how many. She also has socks and hair ribbons to match. She is an only child. I think I know why. If I had a child like Ruby Weber, one would be plenty.

Park School is a big, square two-story brick building that sits on the top of a low, wide hill with lots of green, grassy playgrounds on all sides. They used to have a "boys' side" and a "girls' side" of the playground and you couldn't cross over or you'd get sent inside to sit alone in an empty classroom all recess. It's not like that anymore. The funny thing is that boys and girls still stick pretty much to their own separate territory, but it's nice to know that you don't *have* to.

Just as I expected, Ruby Weber is lying in wait for me at the edge of the school yard. She is wearing a blue and red plaid dress with puffed sleeves, white collar and cuffs, and a tieback sash. It fairly screams "Sears, Roebuck." She is wearing blue socks and a matching blue taffeta hair ribbon. A perfect picture of "Young Miss America on the First Day of School." It's too bad she has such little squinty eyes.

"I see you have a new dress," she greets me. "Did your mother make it?"

"Yes," I said, wondering if I had to be polite and mention *her* new dress. Never mind. She took care of it.

"I have a new dress too," she said, smoothing the skirt down. "Mine came from Sears, Roebuck. Does your mother make *all* your clothes?"

"Yes," I said. "My mother is a gifted seamstress. Doesn't your mother know how to sew?"

Ruby looked confused. The conversation had taken an unexpected twist. Was it possible that wearing homemade clothes was a good thing? She hadn't thought so. She took another look at my made-for-me blue and white dress and couldn't find anything to criticize. She changed the subject.

"We have a new teacher this year."

Now this was news.

"What happened to Miss Tarbot?" I asked. Miss Tarbot had taught sixth grade for as long as I could remember.

"Died," said Ruby flatly, never one to beat around the bush. "How come you didn't know? Didn't you see it in the newspaper?"

"No," I said. "It must have happened while I was in Springfield. Nobody told me."

I was stunned. Miss Tarbot was one of those permanent things like the flag and the multiplication tables. It wasn't that I was especially fond of Miss Tarbot. I hardly knew her. But she had taught Marjy in the sixth grade, and she'd taught Edith, *and she had been going to teach me!*

Ruby had more news.

"Our new teacher is a man."

Things were going from bad to worse. We'd never had a man teacher at Park School. How could you raise your hand and tell a *man* that you wanted to be excused to go to the bathroom? I gave a passing salute to all the boys over the years who had had to ask Miss Tarbot for permission. I pictured the

14

long school year ahead of me, a year of squirming uncomfortably in my seat, torn between asking to be excused and wetting my pants. It was not what I had in mind when I decided to make this a year to remember.

"What's his name?" I asked.

You can tell a lot about a person from his or her name, which is funny because people don't choose their own names. Maybe they just grow to *fit* their names, the way new shoes take on the shape of your feet after a while.

But the fact is that you can have a good name, a bad name, or a medium kind of name, and the name is a kind of picture of who you are. Just tell me how you feel about people named Percy, Elmer, Horace, Dwight, August—or, for that matter, Alma, Bertha, or Ethel? Personally, I don't happen to know anybody with those names and that suits me just fine. Maybe Ruby belongs on that list too.

"So what's this new teacher's name?" I asked Ruby again.

"I don't know," Ruby admitted. "I heard it, but I forgot. It's a long one."

The bell rang then, and the whole school yard began to look like an anthill, with kids streaming in from every corner of the playground and all trying to get in the big double doors of the school at once. I wiggled and squirmed my way into the thick of the jam near the door, and we burst into the hall and exploded in all directions, fanning out to our various classrooms.

I headed up the short flight of broad wooden stairs that led up to the big central first floor hall (still smelling of that red, crumbly sweeping compound that the janitors used to clean the floors!). I noted with satisfaction that everything was still the same. The same floorboards creaked, the same picture of "The Father of Our Country" still hung in its place of honor in the hall, and the very air felt charged with some kind of electricity that said to me "This is where exciting things happen! Something wonderful might happen today!"

The sixth-grade room is on the right, at the head of the stairs. A couple of kids were already there ahead of me. No teacher in sight. I made a beeline for a seat at the front of the room near the teacher's desk and saved the one across the aisle for Peggy. Peggy has been my best friend all through school. She is not at all like Ruby.

Peggy and I don't see each other in the summers. It's always been like this. Both her parents work in a shoe factory, so in the summer they send Peggy off to live with her grandma away out in the country. We don't even write. Three-cent stamps don't come my way very often, and Peggy isn't the letter-writing type anyhow. The telephone? You think our parents would let us talk *long distance*? Not likely. Long distance is for emergency. For serious illness, sudden death, funeral plans. Maybe sometimes to announce family visits, but not for idle chatter, especially the eleven-year-old type. Peggy and I just wait for school to start in the fall and we pick up where we left off in the spring.

It would be good to see her freckled face again. We had a lot of catching up to do. I wanted to tell her all about Jean and Carl in the cornfield, and I was even thinking about telling her about how, this being our last year in Park School, I was planning to do some kind of record-breaking I-don't-know-what project to commemorate my "senior" (so to speak) year. This isn't the kind of thing you tell just anybody. Not Ruby, for instance. But there isn't much I wouldn't tell Peggy.

I kept my eye on the door as one by one the "old regulars" came bouncing, pushing, ambling, or dawdling through the door. Fern, Geraldine, Bonnie, Thomas, Oliver, Betty, Jean, LaVerne, Charles, and Bobby, whom I had marked as "mine" in some special do-nothing-about-it way ever since kindergarten.

There was a new boy, too. He wore white linen knickers.

The room was slowly filling up, but still no Peggy. Soon just about the only empty seat left was the one I was saving. And the only person left without a seat was Ruby, who had been hovering around like a hummingbird looking for a place to land.

"I need a place to sit," said Ruby, eyeing the empty desk across the aisle from me.

"I'm saving that for Peggy," I said.

"Oh, good," said Ruby, "then I can sit there because Peggy won't be coming. Didn't you know she moved?"

"No," I said. "How do you know?"

"I saw her at the movie last week. She's going to West End School this year." Then Ruby smoothed her starched plaid skirt in place and plopped herself down in Peggy's seat.

I felt like somebody had hit me in the solar plexus. Knocked the wind right out of me. No Peggy? My six-years-of-winters best friend? A whole school year with no Peggy in it? Who would I tell secrets to? Who would I choose first in choose-up-sides games? Who would *I* come first with? Who would be my best friend?

Ruby thought she had the answer to that.

"Maybe I'll be your best friend this year," she said.

Yeah, maybe, I thought. Maybe the moon is made of blue cheese. Maybe Santa Claus comes down the chimney. Maybe it snows in July.

I was saved from having to answer her by the arrival of the new teacher.

Chapter Three

HE WAS BIG, this new teacher. Not just big as grown-ups are bigger than children, but six feet tall big. And not fat, but muscle-y and solid-looking, like a football player or a weight lifter. And, I have to say it, handsome.

I probably wouldn't have noticed *that* if it hadn't been for my short summer course in Romance. Jean and the other cousins had taught me some of the finer points of judging male looks. They managed to make it sound a little like judging a dog or a horse, and while it's an awful way to look at a human being, who has a mind and a heart and a soul too, I was helpless against the words they had planted in my head, words like "tall," "dark," "handsome," and "Prince Charming."

Prince Charming was writing his name on the blackboard. He wrote and he wrote and he wrote. "Lawrence W. Van Bellinger." I could see it now: we were never going to get anything done if we had to start every question with "uh . . . Mr. Van Bellinger . . ."

He read my mind. He looked right at me (with his piercing blue eyes!) and said, "You can call me Mr. Van." He meant *all* of us, of course, but it felt as if he were speaking just to me.

I said it over to myself. "Mr. Van." It definitely was one of the good names. Not a Horace or Wilbur or Elmer kind of name.

He didn't *look* like a Wilbur either. He had short, dark curly hair, deep blue eyes, and a romantic-looking blue-black beard shadow.

He dressed differently too. Most of the teachers I'd met so far had been a dowdy lot. The ladies tended to wear shapeless, crepey, slightly rumpled-looking dresses in dullish muddy colors. So wouldn't you expect a man teacher to dress about as smartly? Wrinkled, shiny suit, maybe, and a dingy-white shirt, too tight in the collar? Not Mr. Van. His dark suit was brushed and pressed, his white shirt *white* and starched stiff. He wore what I found out later were French cuffs, with cuff links!

"He looks just like a picture in the Sears, Roebuck catalog," Ruby whispered.

"Does not," I said scornfully, though I had

been thinking just about the same thing.

"I think I'm getting a crush on him," Ruby whispered again.

"Don't be silly," I muttered to Ruby. "He's old. Probably old enough to be your father."

Ruby's hand shot up.

Mr. Van looked down at her. "Yes?" he asked.

"How old are you?" asked Ruby-the-Blunt.

"Twenty-eight," he said, and went on explaining the ground rules for the year.

Of course, it was too bad Miss Tarbot died, but sixth grade with Mr. Van was beginning to look like a whole new kind of world. A definitely improved world. Mr. Van introduced us to the honor system. No more asking for permission to go to the bathroom, for instance. If you needed to go, you just quietly left, and came back promptly.

"I'll give you as much freedom as you can handle," Mr. Van said. "Are there any questions?"

Ruby raised her hand again.

"Are you married?" she asked.

I thought surely this time Ruby had gone too far, but Mr. Van just smiled faintly and answered her as politely as if she'd been a grown-up.

"Yes," he said. "I'm married. I'm six feet two inches tall. I weigh one hundred eighty pounds. I live on Buena Vista Boulevard, and I like reading, baseball, and classical music. Now, let's go around the room and hear from everybody."

Ruby bounced to her feet and announced importantly, "I'm Ruby Weber. I'm eleven years old, four feet eleven inches tall, and when I was born I was so little I could fit into a cigar box. I like tap dancing and new clothes and Sunday School. Would you like to see me tap dance?"

"Uh—yes. Sometime," Mr. Van said. "But first I want to hear from the others in the class."

Ruby sat down, pleased with herself as usual. Her feet under her desk softly tapped out a free sample of what I was sure we'd be seeing more of just as soon as she could get Mr. Van's however reluctant permission.

One by one we all stood up and recited our brief autobiographies. Even shy Freddie blushed his way through a few words with Mr. Van's encouragement. I learned a lot about the kids I'd been going to school with, most of them for six years already. I learned that Fern *called her mother Della!* I learned that Violet Rose has six little brothers and sisters that she has to help take care of, which probably explains why she sometimes smells kind of like a wet diaper. I learned that the new boy's name (the one with the white linen knickers, remember?) was Lance and that he played the violin, but he didn't want to. Norman said his ambition was to be the international marbles champ, and Juanita wanted to play on the boys' softball team because, she said, she was good enough!

Then it was my turn. I had been so interested in what everybody else was saying that I hadn't thought about what I was going to say, and I blurted out the first thing that came to my mind. I started off safely enough with "My name is Emily Ann Campbell and I'm eleven years old." I said I had two younger brothers and two big sisters. Then I just started babbling. I found myself telling the whole class things that I'm not sure I would even have told Peggy if she had been there. "This is my last year at Park School," I said, "and I'd like to do something really special and important this year." Then I added, "When I grow up, I want to be famous."

Now why in the world did I ever say that? It's probably okay to *want* to be famous, unless you're some kind of saint who is supposed to be humble and unselfish all twenty-four hours a day. But to announce it out loud is, well, *lacking in class*. I knew it the minute I said it, and wished I could snatch my words out of the air and cram them back in my mouth. I could feel a deep red blush starting at the bottom of my feet and flooding all over me in a high tide of embarrassment. I sat down suddenly, wishing I were somewhere, anywhere, else.

One by one the rest of the kids in the class stood up and spoke their pieces. I was so wrapped up in my private little world of embarrassment that I hardly heard them. I stared at the ink spot on my desk. It was shaped like an hourglass. My fingers traced the carved initials of some former scholar. I wondered who "C. H." was. I invented names for him: Charles Henderson. Carl Hill. Clifford Howard.

I thought the morning, which had begun so brightly, would never end. No Peggy, and I had already made a complete fool of myself to the new teacher. I could feel the ache in my throat and the burning behind my eyes that signaled I was right on the very edge of bursting into tears. I ducked my head and concentrated on examining the new books we'd be studying this year. A big blue square geography book, a music book with lots of new songs to learn, an arithmetic book with hard-looking problems about trains going at different speeds toward each other and where would they meet, and best of all, a thick new reading book with lots of good stories. At last the ear-shattering bell announced that the long morning was over. I could take my famous little self home for lunch.

Chapter Four

THERE'S SOMETHING FUNNY about Time. It's *elastic*! Sometimes it shrinks and whizzes by, and other times it stretches like a rubber band and it can take an hour for five minutes to pass. I can't prove it, but I've seen it happen time and time again.

That first week of school went by so fast I couldn't believe it. I've always liked school, but Mr. Van made it more exciting than ever, and already I was hoping that the whole *year* wasn't going to take wings and fly clear off the calendar before I had a chance to enjoy it.

The whole day was interesting. I even liked arithmetic now, since Mr. Van made up problems like how many marbles would Norman have if he had a checkerboard with sixty-four squares on it and put one marble on the first square and doubled the number for each square on the checkerboard. (You'd be surprised at the size of the answer you get! It's *big*!) Or he'd ask, if Ruby spent three quarters of an hour tap dancing every Tuesday, Thursday, and Saturday, what percentage of a whole week was that? You never knew who was going to star in the arithmetic problems. But everybody's favorite time was the last half hour of the day when Mr. Van would tell us to put our lessons away and he'd reach for a book and read to us. Right now we were reading *The Adventures of Robin Hood*.

Actually, taking a whole half hour just to read to us wasn't as frivolous as it might seem. I noticed he managed to sneak history, geography, and even arithmetic into the reading. He pulled down the big map on the roller above the blackboard and pointed out where Nottingham and Sherwood Forest were. He had us looking up the Tudor kings and reading about Richard the Lion-Hearted and King John. All of us were making bows and arrows at home and dreaming about the good old days of living in the woods off rabbits and poached deer.

"Is that like 'poached eggs'?" Ruby wanted to know.

Arrgh!

Altogether, Mr. Van kept us so busy that I hardly had time to miss Peggy, but every now and then when I looked across the aisle and saw Ruby sitting in Peggy's seat and preening and retying her already perfect hair ribbon or rearranging her starched skirt, sometimes I would still get a sad, lonesome feeling.

Ruby knew it. She wasn't stupid. Just insensitive.

"Am I your best friend yet?" she asked me almost every day.

I was running out of ways to avoid saying no.

The bell rang for "school's out," and I was gathering up the books I wanted to take home (geography, arithmetic, and *Caddie Woodlawn*) when Mr. Van said, "Everybody dismissed. Except Emily."

A kind of buzz went around the room that was thirty different ways of saying, "Oooooh, Emily! You're in trouble."

I tossed my head and gave the class the scornful look I'd been practicing in case an occasion to use it ever arose. I wasn't worried. My experiences with teachers had always been pleasant ones. He probably wanted to ask me to be the announcer for the P.T.A. program or something like that. Besides, I'd have Mr. Van *all to myself* for a change!

I could see Ruby couldn't quite decide whether she wished she were in my shoes or not, but it was plain that she was curious. She pulled a few delaying tactics, pawing through her poison-neat desk as if in search of something, dropping her books, picking them up slowly, and casting hopeful glances in Mr. Van's direction on the off chance that she might be invited to stay too. When it didn't happen, she trailed reluctantly after the class.

"I'll wait for you," she promised me.

Oh, boy.

I stacked my take-home books on my desk and sat back down in my seat and waited. Mr. Van was sitting at his desk too, writing away in some kind of record book. As he kept on writing, a tiny nibble of doubt began to gnaw at me. Maybe I *was* in trouble. Had I done something? What? Had he seen Norman copying off my spelling test? Then why wasn't *Norman* sitting here worrying?

Just as I was about to say "*I* wasn't cheating," Mr. Van looked up, flashed one of his brilliant smiles, which lit up the room like a Roman candle, and laid his record book aside. Apparently I was right, after all. It didn't look as if I was in trouble.

"I just wanted to talk with you a minute," he said. "You said something interesting the other day about wanting to do something special and important this year, and I thought that sounded exciting."

He paused and seemed to be expecting me to say something. What? I wasn't about to tell him that what I wanted was a plaque above the blackboard that said "Emily Ann Campbell Studied Here."

"I was wondering what kind of thing you had in mind," he said.

More silence.

I *had* to say something.

"I don't know what I had in mind," I confessed at last. "It's just that I've spent six years in this school and when I go I don't want to be forgotten. At least, not right away."

Mr. Van nodded. And quoted:

"Lives of great men all remind us
We can make our lives sublime."

I finished the quotation for him:

"And, departing, leave behind us
Footprints on the sands of time."

"That's it," I said. "I just want to leave some footprints on the sands of time."

Mr. Van nodded. "I guess that's something we all want to do, in one way or another. Well, how are you going to do it?"

I shrugged. This was all beginning to

sound like a very silly idea to me and I wished I hadn't even thought about it, never mind telling the whole class and Mr. Van.

I looked out the window, and I could see Ruby sitting on the wall at the edge of the school yard, patiently waiting for me. For once in my life, I wished I were out there with her.

"Maybe a good way to start is to think about what you do best," Mr. Van continued. "Do you sing? Play a musical instrument? Dance? Draw pictures?"

I cast around blindly for something to say that would satisfy him and end this uncomfortable conversation.

"I write poetry," I heard myself announce. Sometimes I don't know where the words come from that fly out of my mouth. I've never written a poem in my life.

Mr. Van beamed. "You don't say! I don't believe I've ever had a student who was a poet! If you don't mind, I'd like to read some of the poetry you've written. Will you bring me a poem on Monday?"

I was too stunned at the direction this ill-fated conversation had taken to do anything but nod dumbly. As Mr. Van smiled a pleased-looking dismissal, I gathered up my books and walked out into the afternoon sunshine and the almost-welcome company of Ruby.

"Are you in trouble? Did you have to write something on the blackboard a hundred times?" Ruby asked hopefully.

"Ruby Weber," I said, "have you ever known me to have to write anything on the blackboard a hundred times?"

Ruby thought a minute. "No," she admitted. "But what did he want?"

"He just wanted to talk," I said.

"What about?"

"Just stuff," I said:

"Of shoes—and ships—and sealing wax—
Of cabbages—and kings—
And why the sea is boiling hot—
And whether pigs have wings."

Ruby just looked at me, turning that over in her mind. "I have to go now," she said at last. "See you Monday."

"Not if I see you first," I said automatically, and I erased Ruby from my world before she had even turned the corner.

I had a lot to think about. Poetry, for instance. About writing poetry.

Chapter Five

WEEKENDS ARE BUSY at our house. Saturday morning is housecleaning time. Everybody pitches in. We scrub floors on our hands and knees, wax everything that isn't moving, and we don't stop until the whole house is ready for a white-glove inspection. Which it gets. Not from my mother. From my father, who once heard that cleanliness is next to godliness and can't seem to forget it.

After the house is all sparkly and we've recovered from our work, my sister Edith and I clean ourselves up and set off on foot for our weekly trip to the Andrew Carnegie Public Library downtown. Edith is the sister who's three years older than I am. We like to do things together. She's almost as good as a best friend like Peggy, and a whole *lot* better than somebody named Ruby.

Edith and I make this trip almost every

Saturday afternoon. Our house is at the top of a hill, at the very end of a gravel road. Our feet slip and slide on the slick gravel that rolls under our feet as we pick our way down the steep hill. It's a long walk from our house at the edge of town to the library in the very middle. We play games to make the walk seem shorter (don't step on the sidewalk cracks, who can spot the first green car, little boy, woman wearing a hat, man in a blue shirt). At the foot of the hill where the gravel road ends, there's a wide wooden bridge over Goose Creek. We have to run across this because "underneath it is where the troll from *The Three Billy Goats Gruff* lives."

In the wintertime when the walk is not just long, but cold, we are a valiant, dauntless medical team carrying The Serum to ice-bound, epidemic-ridden Sitka. "Mush!" we say to our dog team as we press grimly onward. "Mush!"

It's always dark and cool in the library. We tiptoe and speak in whispers. It's kind of a holy place. If I were in charge of deciding who the saints were, there would be a Saint Andrew Carnegie. I wonder what little kids *do* before they learn to read. For the life of me, I can't remember what was fun when I was two or three or four.

All weekend it was in the back of my mind that I had promised to bring a homemade poem to Mr. Van on Monday, and I still had to write it. I thought about it while we were cleaning house, and I thought about it on the long walk to the library. That was the real stumbling block, the library. Saint Andrew Carnegie tempted me with *Lorna Doone*, and I spent most of the weekend wallowing in the tragic, romantic life of a lady who knew even more about Life and Love than my cousin Jean in her cornfield.

So it was Sunday night before I got around to being a poet. Well, just how hard could it be, writing a poem? There were books and books of them over at Mr. Carnegie's place. *Somebody* had to write them. Though probably not eleven-year-old sixth graders. Maybe I would make history and be the world's first eleven-year-old world-famous poet!

I got out my Big Chief tablet and a sharpened pencil and sat down at the kitchen table. It wasn't the best place in the world to begin a career as a poet. Buddy and Joe-Joe were playing some running, chasing kind of game that brought them tearing through one kitchen door and out the other every few minutes. I could hear the radio playing in the living room and every time I almost had a rhythm worked out in my head, the radio would burst into song in a different rhythm and I'd have to start rhythm hunting all over again. After I stuffed a couple of pieces of cotton in my ears, it went a little better.

Should it be da-DAH-da-DAH-da-DAH-da-DAH, or DAH-da-da-DAH-da-da-DAH-da-da-DAH? Please not *that*. It was the rhythm of *Paul Revere's Ride* . . . "LISten, my CHILdren, and YOU shall HEAR, Of the MIDnight RIDE of PAUL ReVERE."

And what to write *about*? A song from the radio seeped through the cotton balls stuffed in my ears . . . a Gypsy song. That's what I'd write about! Gypsies! They were romantic and poetic and lived a wonderful, happy life just traveling around in their little painted wagons and singing and dancing all day.

I stared at the wall. There was a calendar on it with a picture of Shirley Temple, but that's not what I saw. I saw a Gypsy camp, and I began to write about it.

It didn't all come at once, and there were some scratched-out lines and some words that I wasn't entirely satisfied with, but by the time I had to go to bed, I had a poem.

I copied it over on a clean sheet of paper in my best handwriting.

I Wish I Were a Gypsy

A Gypsy fire is burning
And a Gypsy fiddle sings.
A Gypsy girl is dancing;
In her ears are golden rings.

She wears a skirt of green and red,
Her blouse is gold and blue.
I wish I were a Gypsy girl,
Don't you? Don't you? Don't you?

Well, maybe it wasn't going to make me poet laureate of the world. Maybe it wasn't even as good as the despised *Paul Revere's Ride*. But it was a poem, and I had something to give Mr. Van on Monday.

Chapter Six

IT WAS RAINING when I got up Monday morning, one of those soaking, steady downpours that you know is going to last all day.

"You won't want to walk home at noon," Mama said. "Better take your lunch."

We all scrambled around trying to find something we could pack in a sandwich. Marjy looked over the lunch options and turned up her nose. "I've got some baby-sitting money," she announced, "and I think I'll buy a hot lunch. We have a cafeteria at high school," she reminded us, somehow managing to make it sound as if high school was kind of like the Promised Land beyond the Pearly Gates.

"You can buy hot soup or chili or jello salad or macaroni and cheese or . . ."

Edith and I made faces at her behind Mama's back, and Edith managed to drop the peanut butter knife on a trajectory that left a thin smear of oily goo down the back of Marjy's skirt. We hoped she wouldn't find it until she got to school.

I sliced uneven slabs of homemade bread and spread them with mustard, then fried two eggs until all the yellow part was firm and wouldn't squish and the edges were crisp and brown and curly. Marjy could rhapsodize all she liked about the wonders of a hot lunch of macaroni and cheese and shivery jello salad, but when noontime comes, there's nothing that smells more satisfying and like *real* food than a fried egg sandwich wrapped in wax paper and packaged in newspaper with a string tied around it. I ran down to the cellar where we keep a bushel of red Jonathan apples, tucked one in my pocket, and buttoned my jacket over my books and lunch so they'd stay dry. I debated about wearing the hated galoshes that flapped around my shins, and decided to leave them there tucked down in the bottom of the overshoes box on the back porch where I hoped Mama wouldn't notice them. I took my umbrella and dashed out the door, leaving Edith and Marjy to argue the merits of peanut butter sandwiches versus hot macaroni and cheese.

As I left, Edith (who didn't have any babysitting money) was saying "I *know* what's in my peanut butter sandwich, but do you *really* know what's in that macaroni? Have you ever seen them make it? Do you think those cooks look . . . well . . . *clean?*"

By the time I got to school, I was pretty well soaked, at least from the knees down. Umbrellas are all very well, but they only cover the top half of you. Little rivulets of water dripped down from my skirt and tickled my legs all the way to my ankles. My new school shoes were soaked through and squished with every step I took. They didn't look very new anymore.

So it was going to be one of *those* days, was it? Some days just get off to a bad start and there doesn't seem to be much you can do about it. Things go from bad to worse. I've noticed this before. I wondered what else lay in store for me before the day was over.

I didn't have long to wonder. We had just settled into our seats and then stood up again for the Pledge of Allegiance when there was a rap on the glass door of the classroom. Mr. Van raised his hand for us to hold up on the pledging while he went to answer the door.

I craned my neck to see who it was, and horrors! There stood my father, holding aloft my black, ugly, flapping, buckled, left-at-home galoshes!

"Emily Ann forgot her galoshes," he said, with a look at my soggy shoes and another look at me, which said plainly "We'll talk about this later."

I squirmed with embarrassment. It wasn't just the galoshes, it was having my father at school! Parents don't belong at school. Children and teachers belong at school, and parents belong at home. They are two different worlds, and they don't mix.

Mr. Van said a few words to my father, something about thoughtfulness, and took the ugly galoshes and carried them over to me. I dropped them under my desk and tried to pretend I was somebody else, someplace else. Princess Margaret Rose in Buckingham Palace, maybe. Shirley Temple in Hollywood. Would *their* fathers make them wear ugly galoshes or else carry them to school for all the world to see? I doubted it.

So far, the only right thing about the day was that I had managed to write the poem, in case Mr. Van should ask me for it.

Lunchtime came at last. For the past hour I had been smelling the solid egg-y odor of my sandwich seeping up from inside my desk. It mingled with the baloney and salami and peanut butter smells coming from all parts of the classroom as the room warmed up.

When the noon bell rang, about half the class crowded around the cloakroom in the front of the room, struggled into their damp jackets, and headed for home. Those of us who were left took our lunches out of our desks and spread them out. Some lunches, like mine, were wrapped in last night's newspaper. Some were in neat brown paper bags. Ruby had a red Mickey Mouse lunch box. And a thermos bottle.

Violet Rose didn't have anything.

"Where's your lunch?" Ruby asked her.

That dumb Ruby! Couldn't she tell just by *looking* at Violet Rose in her shabby clothes and too big shoes that if she didn't have a lunch, and if she didn't go home for lunch, it was probably because there wasn't anything in her house to make lunch *out* of, and she was lucky if she'd had anything for breakfast.

"So where's your lunch?" repeated Ruby.

"I don't have any," Violet Rose said softly.

"Why?" persisted Ruby. "Aren't you hungry?"

Emily Ann to the rescue.

"I think I saw you drop your lunch on the way to school," I lied quickly. "I was right behind you, and I thought it was just some junk you were throwing away. If I'd known it was your lunch you'd dropped, I'd have picked it up. Here, have some of my egg sandwich. I can't eat it all." Another lie. I was starving.

Violet Rose thanked me with a look. And eyed my apple wistfully. She got it too.

It was going to be a long afternoon. A long, hungry afternoon.

What else could go wrong with this day?

Probably nothing, I told myself. What else could possibly go wrong? There were only four more hours to go. I had done my homework, and I had my poem written, in case Mr. Van asked for it.

We had geography. We had arithmetic. Then, when it was almost three fifteen and we were all beginning to wonder if Mr. Van hadn't forgotten about our favorite part of the day, he laid aside the arithmetic book, picked up *The Merry Adventures of Robin Hood*, and began to read.

I love that book. I know times were hard for the common person then. Small children were hanged for as little as stealing a loaf of bread because they were hungry. But Robin Hood and his merry men seemed to be having a high old time of it in Sherwood Forest. A kind of never-ending game of outwitting the bad-tempered sheriff of Nottingham. And Mr.

Van read it in such a way that it became a real world to us. Our sixth-grade classroom kind of faded away and we were right back there in Sherwood Forest with Little John and Friar Tuck, roasting our poached venison over an open fire and robbing the rich to give to the poor.

Mr. Van came to the end of the chapter, closed the book with a solid smack, shutting the land of Sherwood Forest inside, and magically we were all back in the sixth-grade classroom of Park School.

"And now we have another treat in store for us," Mr. Van said, smiling at me. "Emily Ann, do you have a poem you'd like to read?"

I wasn't sure how to answer that. I had the poem, all right, but I hadn't thought about reading it to the class. I dug around in my desk and brought it forth.

"Come stand up in front," Mr. Van suggested. "We can hear you better that way."

Still not sure how I felt about this development, I went up and stood beside Mr. Van's desk, cleared my throat, and began to read "I Wish I Were a Gypsy." As I read, I thought it sounded pretty good. Maybe not much better than *Paul Revere's Ride*, but not too bad. When I finished, the class all clapped, and I liked that.

Maybe this day wasn't going to turn out so bad after all.

As the sound of clapping died down, the bell rang and Mr. Van dismissed the class. Everybody ran for the door. I went back to my seat, gathered up my books, and put on my ugly galoshes.

There was nobody left in the room but me and Mr. Van.

"That was a pretty good poem. For a sixth grader," he said. "Have you written any other poems?"

And then the day fell all apart again.

"Oh, yes," I said. "Lots of them."

"Bring me another one tomorrow," he said.

Chapter Seven

WE ALL HAVE CHORES TO DO at home. I have some regular jobs such as peeling potatoes, setting the table, and helping wash the dishes. And then there's another category of jobs called "—and whatever else you are asked to do."

I am not alone in this. Marjy and Edith have jobs too. It's a system that you don't argue with. We've tried. Anyone who complains is very likely to get extra, probably more unpleasant, jobs added to his or her work schedule.

I had extra chores this week. Not because I'd been complaining, but because of not wearing the overshoes that I know I am supposed to wear when it rains.

Daddy had examined my wet new shoes and shook his head.

"Money for new shoes doesn't grow on

trees," he said. "These don't look very new anymore, do they, Emily Ann?"

"No, sir," I said. (A soft answer turneth away wrath. It says that in the Bible.)

It didn't turneth away punishment, however. It was Daddy's opinion that it might help me remember to take better care of my shoes if I would think about shoe care while polishing the shoes of everybody in the family. That's a lot of shoes. And you can probably guess that Daddy's shoe-polishing standards are pretty high. It took me a long time to polish seven pairs of shoes to Daddy's satisfaction.

So, what with homework and all the shoe polishing to do, and the poem to write for Mr. Van, I didn't have much free time Monday night. No seeking out a quiet corner to see what heartrending tragedies were going on in my *Lorna Doone* book. That would have to wait.

I polished the shoes first, then lit into the homework: a page of long-division problems, some reading in the big blue geography book, and going over a list of twenty-five spelling words. I saved this for last because it was the easiest.

I have to *work* at arithmetic, and there's an awful lot about geography that I don't know, but if you *read* how can you not notice how words are spelled? It's like seeing grass every day of your life and not noticing that it's green. Or not registering that snow is white or the sky is blue.

Anyway, once my homework was out of the way, I could use my brain for thinking about poetry.

I've never known any real flesh-and-blood poets, so I don't know how they go about writing. My own way that I've discovered in my recently begun career as a poet is to first have something I want to say, and then try to find the perfect mood and rhythm to say it in. For instance, you wouldn't write a stirring patriotic poem like—say—"The Battle Hymn of the Republic" in the same rhythm you'd use to pen a love poem, would you? I think not. New as I was to this poetry business, nobody had to tell me this.

While I was peeling potatoes, I began running all the poetry I could think of through my head, looking for the right rhythm.

In Xanadu did Kubla Khan
A stately pleasure dome decree

Or maybe:

It was many and many a year ago
In a kingdom by the sea

Or, how about:

The Rainbow comes and goes,
And lovely is the Rose,
The Moon doth with delight
Look round her when the heavens are bare,
Waters on a starry night
Are beautiful and fair . . .

Hmmm. Tricky rhythm.

All through supper I was hearing poetry in my head. I was so full of poetry that supper was almost over before I noticed that I had eaten my way through one of my favorite meals (baked stuffed pork chops, mashed potatoes and gravy, and Mama's home-canned green beans from our summer garden) without even *appreciating* it! What a waste. No telling when we'd have baked pork chops again.

I was still at it while we were doing the dishes. Tennyson, Sir Walter Scott, John Masefield, Matthew Arnold; they tripped through my head from ear to ear, sometimes a few words slipping out of my mouth by mistake.

"What *are* you muttering about?" Edith asked.

I didn't want to say I was about to write a poem. For two reasons. Writing poetry, I'd already discovered, is a very private thing.

Like praying. You don't talk about it. And another thing was, I'd developed a kind of dumb superstition about it. If I announced I was writing a poem, maybe I wouldn't be able to do it.

I was saved from having to answer Edith because she suddenly burst into song. One of the things we Campbells do while we work is sing. We sing a lot. It makes the job go faster, and we very often forget we're working. When Edith sailed into "There's a Long, Long Trail A-Winding . . ." and nudged me to chime in on the alto, I knew poetry hour was over for a while.

It is not possible to sing and write poetry in your head at the same time. In fact, it isn't even possible to listen to someone *else* sing, and write poetry in your head. It's like trying to pat your head and rub your stomach at the same time. Ever tried that? Hard, isn't it?

It also isn't possible to write poetry when two little brothers are playing cops and robbers, or when Marjy is thumping away on the piano at her version of "Annie Laurie" (especially since her version includes playing every third note either sharp or flat and the whole thing in a peculiar bumpy rhythm).

What I needed was a quiet place of my own. An ivory tower.

No wonder Henry Wadsworth Longfellow could churn out so much poetry. I could just imagine his poetry-writing room. A rolltop desk. Floor-to-ceiling shelves full of books. I bet he even had a rhyming dictionary so he didn't have to think up his own rhymes!

I was having such a good time designing Mr. Longfellow's poetry-writing room that we were through doing the dishes almost before I noticed. I gave him Persian carpets on the floor, a big green leather armchair, lots of lamps lighting up the room, stacks of clean white paper, and a jar full of sharpened pencils. Best of all, there was a solid wooden door with a lock on it, so he could keep out noise and company.

Now, where was Emily Ann Campbell, budding poet, going to get a room like that?

Not in this house, I decided, looking around me.

Then I looked out the kitchen door.

We have a big backyard. We live on the edge of town, but a long time ago this used to be way out in the country and the farmers who lived here kept a horse.

I wish we had a horse too, but we don't. We have the next best thing, though. We have the house the horse lived in. The Barn. It's in the far corner of the lot, about as far away from the house as you can get.

It's not one of those big red barns with haylofts and silos and milking machines and all that serious farm machinery, tractors and all that. It's just a little faded-red two-room shed with splintery floors and a rusty corrugated tin roof. But it was empty. It would make a perfect ivory tower.

"Dibs on The Barn!" I shouted.

"Huh?" said Edith, staring at me with a blank look on her face.

"The Barn," I said. "It's mine. I said 'dibs.'"

The United States is governed by the Constitution. Families have their own laws. One of the laws we Campbell kids live by is the Law of Dibs. If you say "dibs" on something, it's yours.

But not always without an argument.

"Hey, wait!" Edith said. "*I* want The Barn! I was planning to use it for a studio and paint pictures."

"Too bad," I said. "I spoke for it first. I said 'dibs.'"

"Well, maybe we could share," Edith bargained.

"No," I said. "The whole idea of The Barn is to be alone. If we shared we might as well stay in the house together."

Then Marjy spoke up from the living room. "I'm the oldest. I ought to get first chance at it. It could be a clubhouse for me and my friends, where we could get away from all the *children* in this house."

And from the withering way she said "children," I was pretty sure she didn't mean Buddy and Joe-Joe.

It's a good thing Mama joined us then. She stood in the doorway and just shook her head from side to side. "What in the world are you girls arguing about?"

We all spoke at once.

"I want The Barn!" (That was Edith.)

"I said 'dibs' on it first!" (That was me.)

"I'm the oldest!" (Marjy.)

"And Emily Ann said 'dibs' first?" Mama asked.

We all nodded.

"Well, then?" said Mama, and waited. Nobody said anything.

Mama sent Marjy off to read a story to Buddy and Joe-Joe. She sent Edith to the cellar to fill a bowl with apples. Then she turned to me.

"I heard why Marjy and Edith want The Barn," she said, "but I missed your reason."

She didn't exactly ask.

I started out by not exactly telling too.

"It would be a quiet place to study," I began. But there she stood, just looking at me with her calm, sweet face, and not telling her anything more would be the same as lying. I just can't lie to Mama. Usually I don't even want to.

"I write poetry," I mumbled. "I need a place to be alone so I can concentrate."

Mama's face lit up like Mr. Van's did when I said that. "Poetry?" she said. "Yes, I can see you would need a quiet place for that."

So The Barn was mine!

I draped my dish towel over the rack under the sink to dry and ran out into the backyard.

I stood in the doorway of The Barn and imagined how it could look. I could hardly wait to get started on turning it into my own private hideaway, but it would have to wait. Right now, the thing I had to do first was write another poem for Mr. Van.

Chapter Eight

MR. VAN BELIEVED in giving rewards.

"That's the way it is in the real world," he said. "It's the people who work hard and do well who get the rewards."

He made a big chart with all our names on it and thumbtacked it to the wall behind his desk. We could get stars for perfect spelling tests, perfect arithmetic homework, and for every extra book report.

"Not fair," complained Norman the Grumbler. "I'll never get a perfect spelling test or arithmetic paper. I won't get any stars after my name."

Mr. Van looked at Norman thoughtfully. "Norman, you have just reminded me of something I left out. Attitude. One of the most important things of all in the real world. And I'm going to make a special deal just with you. Every time you get through a whole day without complaining about something, I'll give you a special gold star all your own."

Norman almost smiled.

Ruby raised her hand. "What are the stars *worth*? Do we get paid for them?"

I squirmed with embarrassment for her. Where did she think the money would come from? Did she think Mr. Van ought to pay us?

Mr. Van just smiled. "There are all kinds of rewards, Ruby. Not all of them come in dollars and cents. The best reward of all is seeing that you do good work."

Ruby didn't look convinced.

As for me, my competitive spirit was rising to the challenge and I was already making plans to rack up so many stars after my name that they'd march right off the chart.

I am not proud of this competitive streak in myself. I keep trying to sit on it by remembering "Blessed are the meek" and "Blessed are the poor in spirit," but the fact is that I am not naturally meek nor poor-spirited.

Apparently Ruby isn't either.

"Emily Ann isn't the only one who can write poetry," she announced suddenly, right out of the blue sky. "I can write poetry too."

Mr. Van turned from the blackboard and gave her a long, questioning look.

"*Can* you?" he asked.

"Yes, indeed," said Ruby. "Want to hear some?"

"I believe I would," said Mr. Van, and he laid the chalk aside and sat down at his desk. "Let's hear one."

Ruby took a sheet of paper from her desk and marched up to the front of the room and began reading:

"Once upon a midnight dreary, while I
pondered, weak and weary,
Over many a quaint and curious volume
of forgotten lore—"

Mr. Van cleared his throat. "Let me see if I can guess the next line," he said. He locked his hands behind his head, leaned back in his chair, closed his eyes, and intoned:

"While I nodded, nearly napping,
suddenly there came a tapping,
As of some one gently rapping,
rapping at my chamber door.
'Tis some visitor,' I muttered, 'tapping at
my chamber door—
Only this, and nothing more.'

"You didn't write that poem, did you, Ruby?"

"Oh, yes, I did," said Ruby. "See? I wrote it in my own handwriting."

"Copied from a book," insisted Mr. Van firmly. "And written by one Edgar Allan Poe, who died about 1849."

"Well, yes," Ruby admitted. "I never *said* I made it up myself. I just said I *wrote* it. Do I get a gold star?"

"I don't think so," said Mr. Van.

Then he went to the star chart, wrote in another name at the bottom of the list, Edgar Allan Poe, and put a gold star by his name.

Ruby didn't seem at all embarrassed, but somehow I knew that Mr. Van wouldn't ask me to read my poem now, and he didn't. I was glad. Edgar Allan Poe is a hard act to follow.

I wasn't home free yet, though. When the bell rang and everybody was grabbing their books and coats and shoving their way to the door, Mr. Van caught my eye and signaled for me to stay behind. I knew what he wanted.

He motioned for me to take a seat, then he held out his hand.

"Okay, let's have it," he said.

I opened my notebook and took out the poem I'd written between supper and bedtime last night. As he read it, I said it over to myself in my mind:

The Summer Gypsy

Does the sun always shine on the
    Gypsies?
Do the moon and stars make all the
    darkness bright?
Do they always dance and sing
Like the bird upon the wing?
Or do they sometimes cry in the night?

Are they always warm and dry in their
    wagons?
Do the Gypsies always have enough to
    eat?
Winter comes with snow and rain,
Does it bring the Gypsies pain?
Do they wish they had a house and bread
    and meat?

I would only want to be a summer Gypsy.
When winter comes, I wouldn't want to
    roam.
When the frost is on the ground
And the snow is all around,
Then I want a warm, snug house to be
    my home.

"Hmmm," said Mr. Van. "I can tell Edgar
Allan Poe didn't write this."

I wasn't sure what he meant. Did he mean he realized that while Ruby might copy poetry out of a book and not give credit to the real author, he recognized my superior code of honor and knew that *I* wouldn't? Or (horrors!), could he mean that it wasn't as *good* as "real" poetry? What was I supposed to say now? Just the simple truth.

"No," I said. "I wrote it."

"Both of the poems you've brought me are about Gypsies," Mr. Van mused. "Any special reason?"

I thought about it. It didn't seem strange to me, or remarkable in any way, to daydream about the Gypsy life. Who *wouldn't* be fascinated by the freedom, the travel, the color, the music? But I suppose what Mr. Van was politely asking was "What do you *really* know about Gypsies?"

Well, actually, I do know a little about them. We live on the edge of town, you know, on a hill, and on the other side of the hill, at the foot, there's a little public park, just a couple of picnic tables and an outdoor fireplace, and in the summer sometimes a small band of Gypsies camps there for a little while.

They scare our neighbors, who say things like "They steal" and "You can't trust them" and "They kidnap children."

They don't scare my mama, though. When the Gypsy women come knocking at our door, bucket in hand, asking for water, Mama sends them back to their camp with water, bread, fresh vegetables from our garden, or whatever else we have plenty of. They are always very polite and never steal anything.

"You'll be sorry," the neighbors warn Mama. But she never has been.

I told Mr. Van about Mama's Gypsies.

"Do you have any poems that aren't about Gypsies?" he asked.

And then I did it again.

"Oh, sure," I said. "Lots and lots of them."

"Bring me some more," said Mr. Van.

Chapter Nine

IT WAS BEGINNING TO LOOK as if my whole life was going to be spent writing poetry. I didn't have time to do anything but my homework, a few household chores, and write poem after poem after poem.

It seemed to me that Mr. Van had developed an insatiable appetite for Emily Ann Campbell's poetry. Every day he asked for another one. And somehow, every day I managed to come up with one for him.

By the end of the week, I had written about Gypsies, death, camel caravans, and old age, none of which I had first-hand knowledge of.

But if I was going to keep up this poem-a-day pace, I was going to need a quiet spot to write. It was time to convert the old barn into my ivory tower.

When Saturday morning came, I got up

early and took a broom, a dust pan, a mop, and a bucket of water out to The Barn and went to work. The old barn hadn't been used in a long time, and the dust flew as I got down to the job.

There were lovely spiderwebs in the corners, and I left them there. They would keep Marjy out. She hates spiders worse than just about anything.

The floor was too splintery to scrub. The mop kept catching on the wood and breaking off long, sharp spears of splinters, so I ended up just sloshing buckets of water across the floor and watching it run down between the cracks and soak into the ground.

When the floor dried I spread out the big piece of carpet that Mama had given me. It nearly covered the floor. The carpet was almost threadbare, but it would keep the splinters from gouging the unwary foot.

Mama gave me an old, cast-off broken-springed easy chair too, which was a surprise every time you sat down in it because you found yourself sinking almost to the floor.

There was a pink wicker table, just right for a desk if you didn't mind that the right front leg was just a little shorter than the other three legs and made the table wobble. I stuck a piece of chewed chewing gum under the short leg and evened it up. At the desk I had a folding wooden chair that said "Property of St. Luke's Episcopal Church" in black stenciled letters on the back. I even had a bookcase made of two orange crates stacked on their sides, one on top of the other.

Everything arranged, I looked around me and saw that it was good. Never mind Mr. Longfellow and his fancy writing room. The Barn was *all mine*, and who knew what wonderful poetry would be written there?

But not right now. I could hear Marjy and Edith calling me to come and pitch in with the Saturday morning housecleaning. Didn't they know I was a poet? Didn't they care that I needed time and quiet to write in? I guess not.

I gathered up the mop, bucket, broom, and dustpan, carried them back to the house, and went to work at polishing up the old homestead. For some reason, sweeping and mopping the family house seemed like a lot more work than cleaning The Barn.

After the house was all clean and passed inspection, I gathered up my schoolbooks, a pad of paper, and a handful of pencils and headed for The Barn.

"Aren't you going to the library with me?" asked Edith.

"Not today," I said. "I've got a lot of homework to do."

Actually, for the first time I could remember, I had forgotten all about our regular Saturday trip to the library. Having The Barn, a place all my own, just drove the library right out of my mind. Well, Mr. Andrew Carnegie's Library wasn't going anywhere. It would always be there. Meanwhile, I had something else to do.

I had to wonder a little why I was spending so much time doing something most people would think of as work. I mean, writing poetry isn't the *easiest* thing in the world. At first, I have to admit, I did it because I just had a choice of either doing it or telling Mr. Van that I was lying when I said I'd written some poetry. Then I had to do it some more because I had given Mr. Van the impression that I not only *could* write poetry, but that I had written *lots* of it. And then, I kept on doing it because I liked having Mr. Van's attention.

But now, it seemed to me that I wasn't writing for Mr. Van anymore. I was writing for myself, because it was something I'd rather do than almost anything else I could think of. There was a newly discovered kind of excitement, a joy in reaching for that little wisp of an idea that floated around in my head, snaring it like a butterfly in a net, capturing it in just the right words, and nailing it down on paper. It filled me with a kind of *energy*. When I'd written a line, a verse, a whole poem that I liked, I felt like running, jumping, singing, dancing, something, anything, to use up that burst of energy that bubbled up in me and overflowed all over the place.

I wondered if Mr. Longfellow felt like this when he wrote *Paul Revere's Ride* or *Evangeline* or *The Song of Hiawatha*. Somehow, I couldn't see dignified-looking Mr. Henry Wadsworth Longfellow leaping around, dancing the joy of creation. Maybe he would sit in that green leather armchair (that *I* had invented for his writing room), cross his long legs, and *smile* with satisfaction. Well, some people are just like that. Me, when I'm happy, I get loud about it!

And then, out of nowhere, I got that happy *writing feeling* and I sort of dived right into it and wrote another poem.

It was a good way to christen The Barn.

Chapter Ten

ONE OF THE REASONS our house seems so small and crowded is that we always seem to have somebody, usually a relative, staying with us "temporarily," which is a piece of time anywhere from two or three days to several months.

Sometimes they're invited and sometimes they're not. Sometimes they just show up on our doorstep, suitcase in hand, like second-cousin Roy who introduced himself with "Betcha don't know me, do ya?" We didn't, but as the weeks passed and he couldn't find a job, we got to know him very well indeed. He finally joined the CCC and went off someplace out West to plant trees for the government.

The traffic was the heaviest at our house when the Depression was at its worst a few years ago. Daddy, being both thankful and proud that he had a job and never had to work for the WPA, the PWA, or take charity, exercised his gratitude by issuing generous invitations to less fortunate relatives to share his (comparative) bounty. This was all very well for Daddy, who could issue his open-handed invitations and sit back and congratulate himself on looking out for his family. It was Mama who had to figure out how to stretch food for seven to feed eight or nine or however many showed up at the dinner table.

Right now, we were down to just one extra guest, Grandpa, and he was one of the "invited" ones.

Grandpa, who is about eighty or a hundred years old, lives alone on the old family farm in the foothills of the Ozarks. He arrived last night for his twice-a-year weeklong visit, chugging up the hill in his old Model T Ford, which was loaded down with an assortment of strange and wonderful presents for everybody . . . for Mama, a hickory-smoked ham that he'd cured himself, for Daddy, a bottle of what Grandpa calls grape juice and Mama calls wine, for Marjy, Edith, and me, little baskets he'd woven out of white oak withes, and for Buddy and Joe-Joe, a baking powder can full of arrowheads that he'd picked up while plowing.

Grandpa was pretty popular with us. He

had laughing blue eyes, a long red beard, and he played the fiddle. Best of all, he was a champion storyteller. Most of his stories were about ghosts and other supernatural beings, and he insisted that they were all as true as gospel. Mama, lady that she is, didn't contradict him, but she did raise her eyebrows, which was a strong statement of contradiction coming from her. It was a great comfort to think of Mama's raised eyebrows when Grandpa got going on one of his tales about long-dead relatives coming back to float spookily around your bed and croak about the way things were on "the other side."

I excused myself from the dinner table (*after* the gooseberry pie, of course) and headed for the back door.

"Where are you going?" Grandpa wanted to know.

I hesitated, sensing some kind of embarrassment trap ahead.

"To The Barn," I said.

"The barn? You got a horse?"

"No."

"A cow! You've got a cow!"

"No, Grandpa."

"Chickens? Ducks? Geese?"

Grandpa wasn't going to quit, was he?

"No, Grandpa. No animals."

"Then why are you going to the barn?"

"Maybe to get out of doing the dishes?" Marjy suggested.

Edith came to my rescue. "She writes there. Poetry. Maybe stories."

Grandpa sipped his coffee and thought that over. It seemed to satisfy him. "Gets it from me," he said. "I'm a first-class story-teller, myself."

As I slipped out the door he was saying, "Did I ever tell you about the time . . ."

And Mama was raising her eyebrows.

When I got to The Barn, I didn't settle down to writing right away. I sat down in my broken-springed easy chair and thought about what Grandpa had said. Where *did* this urge to write come from? Did it really come from Grandpa? I had thought it was something that I had discovered for myself! For the first time, I thought of myself not as being an independent *individual* kind of person, shaped largely *by myself*, but more like a patchwork quilt made up of little pieces handed down from all the ancestors that had come before me.

I wondered what else I would get from Grandpa. His fiddle-playing skill? His taste for "grape juice" (a bit fermented, maybe)? One thing I knew I wouldn't get was his long red beard!

But wait, there wasn't just Grandpa! There was Daddy (would I get his passion for order?), Mama—I hoped I got a *lot* of "quilt pieces" from Mama. And way back, there was great-great-great-great-grandfather Daniel Boone. Did I have a quilt piece or two from him? I thought maybe I could feel a bit of his restless pioneer blood coursing through my veins. Was that why I liked to write about Gypsies and their wandering ways?

Well, it was all something to think about. I sat down at my table, picked up a pencil, and started a new poem. About a patchwork quilt that wasn't really a patchwork quilt.

Chapter Eleven

NOT EVERYBODY WOULD UNDERSTAND what having The Barn, a place all my own, meant to me. They'd think, or even *say*, "What's so great about sitting in a drafty old horse barn, on broken-down furniture, all by yourself?"

Put that way, it *didn't* sound very special, but that's not the way it seemed to me. When I was in The Barn, sitting at my writing table with a pad of paper in front of me, I wasn't Emily-sitting-in-a-drafty-horse-barn. I was a sister to Mr. Longfellow in his writing room, to David the Psalmist, to the troubadours, to all the people I'd ever heard about who liked to put words together in new ways and make them *sing*! It was a *vocation*, kind of like being called to the priesthood!

Try to explain that to Ruby Weber? I guess not. But I bet Mr. Van would understand. I thought about the words I'd say, the way I'd tell him about The Barn—in case I decided to tell him—when I saw him in school on Monday. I could hardly wait for Monday to come.

But when I got to school Monday morning after the barn cleaning, Mr. Van wasn't standing at the door to greet us. He wasn't sitting at his desk grading papers. He wasn't standing at the window looking over the playground. He wasn't anywhere. At least, not anywhere that I could see.

Funny how not having Mr. Van there made it seem like a cloudy day, even though the sun was shining.

In his place was a tall, thin, nervous-looking lady who said in a soft, uncertain voice that she was Miss Humphrey? And she was going to teach us today?

Ruby raised her hand and asked what all of us were wondering. "Where's Mr. Van?"

"I don't know?" asked Miss Humphrey vaguely.

"When will he be back?"

"Tomorrow?" quavered Miss Humphrey.

Well, it could be worse. I was ready to settle down and get to work.

Not everybody seemed to feel that way, though. There are a few kids in every class who feel honor bound to make a substitute teacher wish she'd taken up a different, less hazardous career, like parachuting or sword swallowing.

The persecution of Miss Humphrey began with the pencil dropping, first one, then two, three, six, ten. It's not a very original game, but it's pretty effective.

"Please try to hang onto your pencils?" a wild-eyed Miss Humphrey begged.

The ring leader, Norman, nodded obediently. And dropped his geography book on the floor with a resounding *thwack!* All over the room an epidemic of book dropping broke out.

When nearly every book in the room had been dropped at least once and Miss Humphrey was beginning to twitch, it ceased.

And the foot shuffling began.

By the time afternoon had arrived, even Norman was tired of the game. He had run out of things to drop and was staring vacantly out the window.

Miss Humphrey's hair was all wild looking where she'd been running her hands through it, and she kept looking at the clock about every two minutes.

We were all ready for a change of pace, and we got it.

The door slammed open with a bang, and there on the threshold stood a cowgirl in full regalia. She wore a long denim skirt (slightly soiled), high-heeled boots, (somewhat run-over), a ten-gallon hat (frayed around the edges), and a red bandanna around her neck. She lounged against the doorjamb, snapping her chewing gum and swinging a guitar loosely by its neck. She surveyed us all coolly before announcing, "I've come to sing for you."

Miss Humphrey gave a little gasp of surprise.

So did Violet Rose. "It's my sister," she whispered softly.

We watched in open-mouthed wonder as the cowgirl peeled herself away from the doorjamb and strode to the front of the room where Miss Humphrey fluttered.

"M'name's Mildred," offered the cowgirl, thrusting out a none-too-clean hand. Miss Humphrey, who seemed struck dumb, touched it briefly and retreated toward the windows.

Mildred pursued her.

"What's your'n?" she demanded.

"What? What?" bleated Miss Humphrey in terror.

"Your name! Your name! Who *are* you?" Mildred shouted.

She looked over her shoulder at the class and shrugged. It was obvious to her that she was dealing with an idiot.

Nothing was obvious to Miss Humphrey. She kept mumbling "What? What?" like her needle was stuck, and she had backed herself so tightly up against the windows I was sure that, with any sudden move from Mildred, she was going to levitate to the sill and throw herself out.

Mildred seemed to think so too, and abandoned the chase with, "Well, I can see you're not Mr. Van."

She pulled a tall stool to the middle of her "stage," plopped herself down on it, gave a few tuning tweaks to the guitar pegs, and began her concert.

It lasted the rest of the afternoon. She sang "Cowboy Jack" and "Hobo Bill's Last Ride" and "That Silver-Haired Daddy of Mine" and "Lamp-Lighting Time in the Valley" and then started honoring requests from the floor.

Ruby was waving her hand wildly to get Mildred's attention. At last Mildred nodded to her.

"Would you like for me to tap dance while you sing?" Ruby asked.

Mildred's answer was swift and short.

"No," she said.

Mildred's voice and the school day gave out at about the same time.

Miss Humphrey, left alone, seemed to have

relaxed a little and might even have been enjoying it.

Violet Rose, who usually seemed to be trying for invisibility, was sitting up perkily and basking in reflected glory.

I couldn't help but think that if Mr. Van had been at school, Mildred's concert would have been a lot shorter. In his polite, Sir Galahad way, he would have allowed her one or maybe two numbers, but not a whole valuable afternoon.

I leaned over to whisper to Violet Rose, "Did Mildred know that Mr. Van was going to be absent today?"

Violet Rose gave me a look that in anybody else would be a how-stupid-can-you-be look.

"No. How could she? *We* didn't even know. Mildred's just lucky like that. Things always work out just right for her. Someday Mildred is going to go to Nashville and sing on the Grand Ole Opry. Someday she's going to be rich and famous, and we'll all live in a big white house and eat chicken and ice cream every day."

I hoped Violet Rose was right. I doubted it, but if anybody ever needed something to hope for, it was Violet Rose and family.

What I was hoping for, and I bet Miss Humphrey was too, was that Mr. Van would be back at school tomorrow.

Chapter Twelve

MR. VAN *WAS* BACK AT SCHOOL Tuesday, with a big grin on his face. No wonder. On the blackboard, in big letters and in pink chalk, was the sign: IT'S A GIRL!

What was this? He had a family? He had a wife, we knew that. But now a baby?

It was funny. I simply hadn't thought about Mr. Van having a life of his own away from us. He was always at school when we got there in the morning and he was still there when we left. While I didn't really believe he lived there twenty-four hours a day, I just hadn't thought about his living a part of his life somewhere else.

Maybe he didn't wear a suit and white starched shirt all the time! He probably even ate breakfast and shaved and slept and took baths and—shocking thought!—maybe he even *went to the bathroom* like other people! I closed my mental eyes so I wouldn't see any more pictures like *that!*

Still beaming happily, Mr. Van called the class to order and went through the motions of opening exercises, the salute to the flag, and singing "America." Then, before getting down to the business of arithmetic, he perched on the edge of his desk and told us about his new baby.

"She weighs seven pounds and is twenty inches long," he said.

That didn't mean much to me. Was that good? Was that bad? I didn't know. I didn't have anything to compare it with.

Ruby did. Herself, of course.

"*I* only weighed three and a half pounds," she said proudly. "The doctors all said it was a miracle I lived."

I could think of some other word besides "miracle." Like "pity," maybe.

And leave it to Ruby to turn the spotlight on herself. This was *Mr. Van's baby* we were talking about. Time to step in before Ruby started in on her story about "I was so little I could sleep in a cigar box."

"What's your baby's name?" I asked Mr. Van.

"Mary," said Mr. Van. And the way he said it you'd have thought he invented the name instead of choosing about the commonest name in the whole world.

"It's her mother's name too," he explained.

I sighed silently. Mr. Van's family was going to be in for a lot of confusion. I wished he'd consulted me before it was too late. We'd already had that situation in our family. My grandpa's name is Homer. My uncle's name is Homer. My cousin's name is Homer. You get all three of them in the same room, which happens pretty often, and every time somebody says "Homer" three people answer.

It would have been better if Mr. Van had named his daughter—oh, *Emily*, for instance!

I guess I don't have to mention that we didn't get a lot of schoolwork done that day. Mr. Van was trying hard, but we could all see that he was still wrapped up in his new role as Little Mary's father and was having a hard time keeping his mind on reading, writing, and arithmetic.

As for the rest of us, we were still a little off balance too, from yesterday's double dose of fluttery Miss Humphrey and forceful Mildred-the-Songbird.

Violet Rose seemed to be the only one in the room who looked and acted like herself. In fact, she even looked better than usual. Sure, her dress was as ragged and faded as ever, and her shoes were the same too big hand-me-downs she always wore, but she was sitting up proudly and held her head high. And she seemed to have recovered from a lifelong case of shyness.

When Mr. Van asked us what we did yesterday afternoon, Violet Rose's hand was the first one up, beating out Ruby by a good tenth of a second.

"We had music!" said Violet Rose. "My sister Mildred brought her guitar and sang for us! All afternoon!"

"Oh, my," said Mr. Van. "That must have been—very nice."

"Yes, it was," agreed Violet Rose. "Mildred is going to be a big star someday. Probably pretty soon. She'll be on the Grand Ole Opry, and we'll all move to Nashville and live in a big white house."

"She must be very good," Mr. Van said kindly. "I'm sorry I missed her concert."

"Maybe she could come again," Violet Rose offered.

"We'll see. We'll see," Mr. Van said.

"Mildred, Mildred, Mildred," muttered Ruby. She raised her hand and waved it noisily.

"Yes, Ruby?"

"I have an aunt who can sing both soprano and alto!" she announced.

Violet Rose wasn't impressed. "Mildred can too."

"Well, my aunt can sing them *both at the same time!*" Ruby said firmly.

We all thought that over.

Mr. Van cleared his throat and reached for a geography book.

Usually I don't have any trouble falling asleep. I curl up in my warm, cozy bed with the quilts and comforter pulled up to my ears, and I'm asleep almost before my head hits the pillow. I don't even hear the murmured singsong of Edith and Marjy in their bunk beds across the room comparing the events of their day, nor the mournful wail of the screech owl that lives in the woods, nor the drunken singing of old Harley Kincaid as he lurches through our backyard with his hound dog and gun on his way coon hunting.

He just sings one song, about how he's going to lay his head on a lonesome railroad track and let the two-thirty train erase his troubled mind. I haven't heard him often (I'm usually asleep) and I guess he just knows that one song, though maybe he could get rich and famous in Nashville too, just like Mildred. But I think he'd rather be coon hunting and drinking and singing to the moon and the screech owl.

I hate it when I go right to sleep. Night is such a good time for thinking and imagining things. Sometimes I pretend I'm an only child, an orphan, being raised by a rich old aunt. (I don't have any rich old aunts. There aren't any rich old *anybodies* in my family!) I imagine the house I'm living in, a big, old graystone house with round towers on the corners. One of the tower rooms is mine, of course. It has a window seat all around it and casement windows that look out on a wide, grand boulevard. The tower room is just a part of my private suite; I also have a bedroom and my own bathroom. With a sunken marble tub. My bedroom has a thick, soft white carpet so deep your feet sink in up to your ankles, and there is a big bed in a corner, a bed so high you have to climb up some little steps to get in it. The bed is all closed in with wooden sliding panels, like a little room, and one of the bed walls is a floor-to-ceiling bookcase. I can climb into my big high bed, turn on a built-in lamp, reach for a book, and *read all night*. Usually I don't get much further than this because I either fall asleep or I get homesick for my real house and family and erase my dream world!

Tonight I lay awake, long after Marjy and Edith had ended their nightly whispers and gone to sleep. I stared into the dark and thought about Mr. Van's other life, the life he led on Buena Vista Boulevard where there was a woman named Mary, and now Little Mary. I wondered what it would be like to be part of that family, to live in the same house with Mr. Van. Who would I rather be, Big Mary or Little Mary?

Whoa! I thought. *What's going on here?* Another picture flashed into my mind, Jean and Carl last summer, kissing in the cornfield and every other place they got a chance. Now why was I thinking about Jean and Carl and Romance?

I certainly didn't want to be standing out in a cornfield with Mr. Van, kissing him. Did I? I couldn't even imagine it. I just wanted to be where he was, to see him, to hear him talk, to have him smile at me. What did it all mean?

Listen, Emily Ann Campbell, I told myself. Mr. Van is your *teacher!* He is twenty-eight years old. He is married. He is a *father! You* are eleven years old. You're not even *finished* yet! Eleven-year-olds don't fall in love. You are not in love.

But it didn't do any good. I knew I loved Mr. Van. That I would always love him, and that I would never love anybody else for the rest of my life.

Chapter Thirteen

BEING IN LOVE was affecting my poetry writing. I wasn't writing about Gypsies or death or nature anymore. All my poems seemed to have something to do with L-o-v-e. And I didn't want anybody to see them. I especially didn't want Mr. Van to see them.

But he kept asking. Almost every day he asked. Finally he cornered me at recess on the playground as I was heading for the tree where Fern and Bonnie and Geraldine were waiting.

"Emily Ann," he said, "I haven't had a new poem for a whole week. You haven't stopped writing, have you?"

I couldn't lie to Mr. Van.

"No," I said, and started to drift away.

He put out a hand and stopped me.

"Bring me one tomorrow," he said. "That's an assignment."

He smiled, but I knew he meant it.

Anyway, I wanted to do what Mr. Van asked. I wanted to please him. I wanted to make him happy. I wanted to give him little presents. He could have had anything of mine he wanted.

My Shirley Temple paper dolls? Of course!

My little penknife shaped like a lady's boot? Certainly!

My head on a silver salver? Coming up!

But what he wanted was poetry.

Well, there was just no way out of it. I was going to have to go straight home after school and write a new poem that I could show him without blushing.

It wasn't that easy.

My time is not always my own once I get home. It's "Will you run to the store and get a quart of milk?" or "It's time to set the table" or "Can you keep an eye on Buddy and Joe-Joe while I take this soup to Mrs. Murray?"

By the time all the "can you's" were taken care of, it was nearly supper time and beginning to get dark.

I slipped out the back door and ran to The Barn. There isn't any heat in The Barn so I kept my coat on. I considered keeping my mittens on as well, but it's pretty hard to handle a pencil and paper when you're wearing mittens.

The lighting was poor too. There wasn't

any electricity and Mama wouldn't let me have a kerosene lamp there.

"Too dangerous," she explained. "Fires."

I reminded her that I was a Girl Scout and Girl Scouts know all kinds of ways to prevent fires.

"Well, here's one more way to add to your collection," Mama said. "Don't take a kerosene lamp to The Barn."

So all I had was a big flashlight and the batteries were getting weak.

I thought and scribbled and scratched lines out and chewed on the end of my pencil, but the dark and the cold drove me back into the house before my poem was finished.

The disturbing thing was that this poem seemed to follow the pattern of most of the other poems I'd been writing lately. I couldn't seem to help myself. Anybody could tell I was writing about L-o-v-e again.

I finished writing it after supper and the dishes were done. I read it over to myself:

Sir Galahad Rides Again

Today I saw Sir Galahad,
He wasn't wearing armor,
Nor saving a fair maiden
From a dragon that might harm her.

He wasn't with a band of knights,
He didn't ride a horse.
You ask me if I'm sure 'twas he?
I answer, "Yes, of course!"

I knew him by his noble deeds,
His eyes were kind and bright;
He's looking for the Holy Grail—
I'm looking for a knight!

It wasn't a poem I was eager to show Mr. Van, but I didn't have any new ones that weren't about L-o-v-e. It would have to do. I put it with my schoolbooks and went to bed.

I was glad about one thing. Mr. Van had stopped asking me to read my poems to the whole class. He was the only audience these days. Sometimes he read my poetry during recess, sometimes he asked me to stay a few minutes after school.

The final bell of the day had rung and we were all crowding toward the door. Mr. Van had forgotten all about me. I couldn't decide if I was relieved or disappointed.

I didn't make it to the door.

"Emily Ann! Remain here, please." Mr. Van motioned me back to my seat.

When the last sixth grader had passed out the door and the school was beginning to quiet down, I handed Mr. Van the poem. I watched his face as he read it once, and then again. Did he like it? Did he hate it? Would he guess that it was about him, that he was my Sir Galahad?

At last he raised his eyes and looked across the desk at me. He smiled. "It's not about anybody real, is it? Not Bobby, for instance?"

Good. I didn't have to lie. "No," I said. "It's not about Bobby."

"Hmmmm," he said. "How old are you, Emily?"

"Almost twelve," I said.

He looked at me thoughtfully again. He couldn't read my mind, could he? Was it written all over my face that the poem was about *him*?

Apparently not, thank goodness.

"It's a pretty good poem," he said at last, "for an eleven-year-old. Keep up the good work."

Then he put the poem in a folder in his desk, and my feet hardly touched the floor as I floated happily out the door.

Chapter Fourteen

IT WAS SATURDAY AFTERNOON, and warm for December. The house was clean, and Edith and I had just returned from our weekly trip to the library. I carried my library books out to The Barn for a couple of hours of peaceful, uninterrupted reading. Libraries bring out a greedy streak in me. The look, the feel, the very *weight* of an interesting-looking, unread book make me happier and more excited than just about anything I can think of. I want to gobble the whole book down at once, to feed the starving reader inside me!

This week I had chosen *Wuthering Heights*, which I loved, *The Scottish Chiefs*, which I loved even more, and *Rob Roy*, which turned out to be a mistake. Nobody told me how *wordy* Sir Walter Scott was. I'm sure there's a story in there somewhere, probably a pretty exciting one too, but right now I don't have the patience to hunt for it.

When I'm in The Barn, I'm not always writing. Sometimes I'm reading. Sometimes I just sit in that broken-springed easy chair and think about things.

I think about "How do they *know* the world is really round?" (Looks flat to me.) And I think about "How come God spoke to Moses out of a burning bush—and hasn't been heard from lately?" And I think "If the world really *is* round, I bet I could dig through to China."

And lately I'd found myself thinking a lot about Violet Rose. It just didn't seem fair that somebody as nice as Violet Rose had such a hard life. Why should she go hungry and have to wear ragged hand-me-down clothes while others—oh, Ruby, for instance—had closets full of new dresses and all kinds of extra fancy things like the Mickey Mouse lunch box and Thermos bottle?

If this were a story, a fairy godmother would appear and shower Violet Rose with all the good things she deserved, or at least a few of the things she needed.

But without a fairy godmother, it looked as if Violet Rose was just going to have to struggle along on her own and be poor and hungry until her sister Mildred made them all rich and famous at the Grand Ole Opry in Nashville, which I doubted would happen in the near future, if at all.

I played around for a while with the idea of what I would do if I were Violet Rose's fairy godmother. I'd give her some pretty new clothes. Shoes too. And soap. Not just plain soap or she might think I was hinting at something, but fancy, good-smelling soap and a pretty tin of talcum powder. And a picnic basket full of food like oranges and ham and candy and cheese and crackers and cans of soup. A loaf of Mama's homemade bread. Some sausage from Grandpa's farm. Eggs too. A jar of Mama's damson plum jam.

Thinking of all that food made me hungry. "Must be about time for supper," I decided, and headed for the house.

Mama was making noodles for soup. I sat down at the kitchen table and watched her roll the dough out on the floured bread board and cut it into thin, even strips.

"How would you like to be a fairy god-mother?" I asked her.

"Who wouldn't want to be a fairy god-mother?" she asked. "What can I do for you, Cinderella?"

"Not me," I said. "I'm not Cinderella. Violet Rose is. She doesn't have anything. I wish we could give her food and clothes and hair ribbons and money."

"Hmmmm," said Mama. "Fairy godmothers have to be pretty careful. I wouldn't want to embarrass Violet Rose."

"Yeah," I said. "I mean 'yes.'" (Mama doesn't like it when we use slang. She says it hurts her ears.) "Maybe Violet Rose could have a *secret* fairy godmother."

"Maybe," said Mama. "I'll help you think about it. Why don't you ask Violet Rose to come over after school sometime? You haven't had anybody over to play since—for a long time."

I knew she had almost said "since Peggy moved away." A little cloud moved across my world. I still missed Peggy.

"Violet Rose is awfully busy helping out at home," I said worriedly. "But maybe her sister Mildred could stop playing her guitar long enough to help take care of the little kids and give Violet Rose a break. I'll ask her."

Monday, at recess, I waited until Violet Rose was alone to invite her over. I didn't want Ruby to overhear and offer to come too.

Violet Rose looked happy at the invitation. "I can't come today. I have to ask my mom first. Maybe I could come tomorrow."

"Okay," I said. "Tomorrow will be fine."

When I brought her home Tuesday, Mama had two glasses of milk and two little plates set out on the kitchen table. I usually just have a couple of cookies or an apple, but Mama had made a plate of peanut butter and jelly sandwiches and oatmeal cookies with raisins and black walnuts in them. Violet Rose appreciated them. That is what's known as an understatement. You wouldn't believe anyone as small as Violet Rose could put away so many sandwiches and cookies. I tried to eat my share so she wouldn't feel awkward, but I couldn't keep up with her.

While we were eating, Mama was sitting at the end of the table, with her sewing basket out, and she was pawing through her bag of quilting material. Mama doesn't have much spare time, but when she does, she likes to piece quilts. She uses leftover scraps from the dresses she makes us, and sometimes from clothes we've outgrown, if they aren't too faded.

She was holding up one of my dresses that I wore last summer. She was talking to herself. "This dress is still too good to cut up for quilt pieces. Pity not to get more use out of it. Are you *sure* you can't get into this anymore, Emily Ann?" she asked.

"I'm sure," I said, "and it's too bad,

because that was one of my favorite dresses."

Mama started to stuff it back into the rag-bag. Then she looked over at Violet Rose and seemed to be measuring her with her eyes. "Would you come over here a moment, Violet Rose?" she asked.

Violet Rose got up and went over to stand beside Mama. Mama shook out the wrinkled pink cotton dress and held it up against Violet Rose. "Looks like it might fit you just fine. I don't suppose you could use another dress, could you?" she asked. "It seems such a pity to have it go to waste. You'd be doing me a big favor. That is, if you don't mind that it's already been worn."

"I don't mind," said Violet Rose softly. "I always wear hand-me-downs. And this is a real pretty one." She hugged the dress to her, and her hands patted and smoothed it gently, almost reverently.

"Well, that's that, then," said Mama. She dug around in the bag. "Here's another one. Might as well take it too." She pulled out a green and white dress with a little matching bolero jacket. Bolero jackets had been popular last year, and I'd loved that dress.

"I'll just run the iron over them and put them in this paper bag for you," Mama said.

Violet Rose looked really happy. We put

our empty plates and glasses in the sink, and I took her off to show her The Barn.

I'd never invited anybody into The Barn before. I didn't tell her it was my answer to Mr. Longfellow's writing room. I told her it was a place where I could be alone when I felt like it. Violet Rose was enchanted.

"It must be nice to have a place all your own," she said.

I expect she was thinking about all those little brothers and sisters she had.

When it was time for Violet Rose to go home, I went in the house to get the bag with the dresses in it. It was heavy. I could tell it held more than just two dresses. I peeked inside. Underneath the ironed and neatly folded dresses Mama had added a loaf of her good homemade bread, a big piece of hickory-smoked ham from Grandpa's farm, and a bag of the oatmeal cookies, enough for all Violet Rose's little brothers and sisters.

My mama could put fairy godmothers out of business. She made me feel so good that after Violet Rose had thanked Mama and gone home, I went back to The Barn and wrote a poem about "My Mama, the Fairy Godmother."

I knew it wasn't a great poem, but Mama liked it.

Chapter Fifteen

IT WAS A COLD WINTER. We didn't have a lot of snow. Sometimes we don't. But the ground freezes and there's frost on the windowpanes in the morning. A cold, wet wind chapped our cheeks and numbed our toes on the cold walk to school.

Thawing out in the warm schoolroom was a mixed pleasure. As the circulation returned to my numbed feet and legs, it was like being tortured with hundreds of tiny pinpricks. I envied the girls whose parents let them wear snow pants, and I grumbled mentally at the hard-heartedness of a father who put ladylike appearance above his daughters' comfort. Maybe even their *health!* When I got pneumonia, he'd be sorry. Maybe I'd forgive him in a touching deathbed scene.

"Oh, *why* didn't I let you wear snow pants?" he'd repent tearfully.

I wasn't the only one not dressed for the cold. Violet Rose was wearing my old summer dresses, but she wasn't complaining. It was an improvement over what she'd worn before. (Happily, Ruby hadn't recognized them. Can you imagine what she'd say if she had?)

For a few weeks it had been too cold for me to spend much time in The Barn, but that was good in a way, because I discovered that I had tapped into a new level of concentration and could write wherever I was, no matter what was going on around me. Well, almost. Especially if I stuffed cotton in my ears. Marjy and Edith had taken to amusing themselves by talking about me right in front of me and laughing when I didn't even hear them.

What I missed, though, was the Saturday trips to the library. It was just too cold to make the long walk there, and I was hungering for something new and good to read. I had read almost all the books in the school library and the few things we had at home. I was reduced to reading a book about birds, an old Boy Scout Handbook, and instructions on "How to Play the Guitar." (You think I had a guitar? Wrong. Just the book.) I was even eyeing the Bible in desperation.

Actually, I like lots of the Bible. The psalms, for instance. Pure poetry. And all the stories about David, who is my favorite character. Isaiah is good. Proverbs. Forget Revelation. I've tried to read that, and I will have to be very, very book hungry before I try it again.

One Saturday in late January, we woke up to spring in the air. The January thaw. The frozen ground was softening, frost had melted, the sun was shining, and the air smelled warm and sweet.

Edith and I stuck our heads out the door, nodded to each other, and said, "Library today!"

We hurried through the Saturday morning housecleaning and got out of the house well before noon.

Everything in the library looked the same. It was like coming home again. Nothing had changed. Old men sat at the tables reading newspapers on sticks and clearing their throats. Women with blue-white hair clustered around the romance fiction.

It was so quiet you could hear the measured tick of the grandfather clock in the corner.

I headed for the fiction section, and Edith went to look for books on art and painting.

I had narrowed my choices down to four, which was all I could carry comfortably for any distance, when Edith came hurrying back with a strange look on her face.

"What?" I asked.

"There's somebody . . . there's somebody—" she stammered. She couldn't seem to finish the sentence.

There's somebody *what?* I wondered. Throwing a fit? Giving away candy? With two heads? Selling balloons?

"Where?" I asked.

She pointed to the door.

I looked at the door. Nothing.

Edith shook her head. "Farther."

I looked toward the foyer, the little entry between the outside door and the inside door. There was somebody there all right, an older girl, somebody I didn't recognize. She was leaning against the wall and looking out the door to the street. Nobody I knew.

But wait. There was something about her, something familiar about the way she held her head, tapped her foot.

I drew closer, slipped through the inner door of the foyer, and took a better look.

"Peggy? Is that you, Peggy?"

The "older girl" turned around. She looked at me and grinned.

"Yeah, it's me, all right."

Well, it was and it wasn't.

She looked a lot more grown-up than the Peggy I remembered. Nail polish. A frizzy permanent. And there was something missing . . . the freckles! Where were the freckles? Makeup! Twelve-year-old Peggy was wearing *makeup!* Even lipstick. But I told myself that underneath all that "cake icing" it was still Peggy.

I started talking fast, to catch her up on what things were like this year at Park School. I told her that Miss Tarbot had gone to her reward. I told her about Mr. Van, how he reminded me of Sir Galahad. I told her that Ruby Weber was still as big a pain in the neck as ever. I told her that Violet Rose was probably as good a friend as I had this year.

But even though we hadn't seen each other in eight months, I couldn't seem to hold Peggy's attention. All the time we were talking, she just cracked her chewing gum and kept looking out at the street.

I finally asked her, "What are you looking at?"

"Nothing," said Peggy. "I'm just waiting for Wally. We're going to a movie."

"A date?" I blurted out. "You've got a date? With a boy?"

Peggy grinned. "Sure. Who else would I have a date with? Don't you go out with boys?"

I shook my head. I know I'm not going to be allowed to go out with boys until I am at least sixteen. Maybe older.

"Do you—do you, you know, hold hands and stuff?" I asked.

"And stuff," Peggy said. "We're going to sit in the back row of the balcony. Wally says it's more romantic there."

There was that word again, romantic. It seemed to me that ever since last summer, Romance kept cropping up everywhere I looked, like dandelions in the spring. I'd never even *thought* about Romance before that. Was it *me*, or was the whole world suddenly turning into a kind of huge romantic swamp, dangerously like quicksand?

I didn't have much time to brood about it, though, as Peggy's bright eyes spotted Wally on the way up the steps, and she turned to me hurriedly. "I gotta go. Here's Wally. I'll be seeing you, Emily."

I gave the correct response, "Not if I see you first," but I said it to her back. She was gone.

I just stood there in the lobby watching Peggy and Wally walk away together, giggling and pushing at each other. She didn't even look back once.

It was worse than not seeing her at all. It

was as if the old Peggy had died. I knew I'd never see *my* Peggy again.

"Good-bye, Peggy," I said to myself. "Good-bye."

I guess it had been in the back of my mind all along that someday, somehow, Peggy would *come back*, but I could see now that it wasn't going to happen. It couldn't. Even if she moved back, right next door to me, she had changed. Or I had changed. And nothing would ever be the same again.

It was so sad, so crushingly, blackly tragic I didn't know how I was going to make it all the way home without bursting into loud, embarrassing sobs. I was glad Edith knew enough not to try to talk to me or make me feel better.

When we got home at last, I headed straight for The Barn. There was only one way I could think of to bury the lost Peggy. I would turn her into a poem.

Chapter Sixteen

The year was going by too fast. (Emily Ann's Law of Elastic Time, remember?). Every time I flipped a page over on the calendar, I was reminded that the time was coming closer when I would no longer be in sixth grade, basking in the sunshine of Mr. Van's presence.

Not only that, I didn't seem to be making much progress toward leaving any "footprints on the sands of time." True, I had a satisfactory number of stars for good homework on our star chart, but so did a lot of other people (including *Norman*, I am happy to say!), and it certainly wasn't enough to get me that plaque above the blackboard saying "Emily Campbell Studied Here." (I was always just kidding about that. Kind of.)

I asked Mama once about the best way to go about getting famous, and she said she thought people didn't get famous *all at once*, but that it was an accumulation of lots of little things done well that added up, but I didn't see how even ten years of perfect spelling papers was going to put me in the history books. As a matter of fact, I didn't even think about it very much anymore. There was too much interesting stuff going on.

Valentine's Day was coming up already. At home, in a romantic mood, I "borrowed" Marjy's red lipstick (that she isn't allowed to wear) and drew a big red heart on the February page of the calendar in our room.

When Marjy saw it, she was furious but couldn't make much of a fuss since officially she doesn't *own* any makeup. She knew who did it, though. The next morning when I went to get dressed, I found every pair of socks and underpants I owned had been tied into tight knots. It took me so long to untie enough clothes to wear that I had to run all the way to school.

In the weekly art class, we had all had a hand in making the valentine box that stood on the filing cabinet next to Mr. Van's desk. Underneath, it was just a plain brown cardboard box, but we had covered it with white crepe paper and tied it up with red crepe paper ribbons and pasted big and little red hearts all over it. I thought it looked very romantic. More romantic than valentine boxes of previous school years? I don't know. Maybe it was just me. Ever since last summer I seemed to see Romance in just about everything.

When I was younger (like in fifth grade), Valentine's Day was just a competitive event, a numbers game, a popularity contest to see who could get the most valentines.

This year it seemed different. I found myself thinking not so much on "how many?" but "who from?" Would Bobby send me one this year? Would he sign it "Love"? And did I really care? I wasn't sure. Would Mr. Van give us valentines?

Somehow I knew that even if Mr. Van did give us valentines, he'd give them to *everybody*. And they would be just the friendly teacher-to-student kind. And mine would be just like everybody else's. His wife, Mary, and Little Mary would be the ones who got the lacy, mushy, sentimental kind. Probably candy and flowers too. I hoped they realized how lucky they were.

At recess Ruby sought me out and she jingled when she walked. In fact, she seemed to make a point of bouncing up and down, and the more she bounced, the more she jingled. I could tell she was dying for me to ask what the jingling noise was. When I didn't say anything, she took a handful of change out of her pocket and let it fall in a clinking stream from one hand to the other, a glittering shower of nickles, dimes, and pennies.

"I'm going to buy my valentines after school," she announced. "I've got a whole dollar. How much do you have?"

I didn't have anything yet. I was pretty sure I wouldn't get as much as a dollar, but I didn't want to tell Ruby that. I didn't have to. She went on with the conversation all by herself.

Sometimes Ruby's looks are more eloquent than words. Her beady eyes lingered on my homemade dress, and I knew what she was going to say before she said it.

"I suppose you're going to *make* your valentines."

I hadn't even thought of that. It was a good idea, even if it came from Ruby.

"I might," I said. "I haven't decided yet."

The more I thought about it, the better the idea sounded. For one thing, it would cost a lot less. All I had to do was get some red art paper. I thought we might even have some at home. I could get some lacy white paper doilies, or even use scraps of real lace, or make folded, cutout lace from plain white paper.

But the main thing was that it would be so much fun. I could make the valentines say exactly what I wanted them to say instead of just trying to make the ready-made, store-bought sentiments fit everybody. My fingers were itching to begin.

That night after the supper dishes were done, I gathered up everything I could find that looked like part of a valentine and spread my stuff out on the big kitchen table. I had some red construction paper, some white tissue paper from a shoe box, some scraps of lace and rickrack from Mama's sewing basket, some gold foil saved from an old box of candy, a seed catalog with lovely colored flower pictures, scissors, and some paste made from flour and water.

Marjy eyed my material with disdain.

"Making your own valentines? Nobody likes homemade valentines."

"They'll like mine," I said. "Mine are going to be special."

And they were. Some of them, at least. For Violet Rose, I found a perfect violet and a perfect rose in the garden catalog. For Fern I found—you guessed it—a fern! They weren't all that easy. Some of them were just ordinary "Be My Valentine" cards with your standard, everyday heart and paper cutout lace.

It was getting late by the time I got around to Ruby's, she being alphabetically last.

I had been working hard and seriously and was ready now for a little fun. Almost as if it had a life of its own, my pen dashed off a verse for Ruby's valentine:

Mirror, mirror on the wall,
Who's the smallest of us all?
Tiny feet (of which she's vain),
Tiny heart and tiny brain.
Mirror, if I ask you sweetly
Could she disappear completely?

I copied the smart-alecky verse on a thick piece of white paper. I cut a tinfoil circle for a mirror. I pasted a few crooked and misshapen hearts around the edges and wrote "For Ruby Weber" at the top.

Did I dare put it in the valentine box? Probably not. Did I really want to? I wasn't sure. I yawned. Time to go to bed. I'd make up my mind tomorrow.

I gathered up all the scraps of paper and washed out the paste dish, put the scissors away and put my valentines in a paper bag beside my books and homework, and went to bed.

I got to school early the next morning. I

often do. I like to settle in, maybe browse in the bookshelves and have a few minutes of quiet between the hurry and noise of home and the hurry and noise of a roomful of classmates.

Today Ruby was there ahead of me. She had all her valentines spread out on her desk and was admiring them. They did look impressive, some of them with red honeycomb hearts, others with moving parts, and all of them expensive looking.

"Let me see yours!" she demanded.

"No," I said. "They're supposed to be a surprise. You can wait two more days to see them." Then, knowing how persistent Ruby can be, I quickly took my valentines out of the paper sack and stuffed them through the slot in the valentine box.

Teachers must really hate the day or two before a big holiday (and I rank Valentine's Day way up on the holiday scale just below Christmas and Easter). There's a kind of explosive energy afoot that makes concentrating on reading, writing, and arithmetic hard. You could practically feel the room hum and buzz. It was like that all morning and hadn't gotten any calmer when I got back from lunch.

By three thirty we were all like caged animals waiting for release. Even Mr. Van.

Maybe especially Mr. Van. When the bell rang, we were off and running. Everybody except me. Mr. Van had said again, "Everyone excused, except Emily."

Ruby gave me another one of her pitying looks. It was hopeless. Wasn't she ever going to learn that when Emily Ann Campbell was asked to stay after school it wasn't because she was in trouble?

Except maybe this time Ruby was right.

Mr. Van was looking very serious. No smiles. No friendly nods. He didn't even look at me until the last kid had left the room and the glass-paned door closed behind her. Then he looked at me a long time before he said anything.

He reached under the blotter on his desk and pulled something out. A valentine.

My stomach gave a sickening lurch. I recognized it at once. It was the valentine I'd made for Ruby.

"Did you make this, Emily?" he asked.

(I hadn't signed it, but he knew it was my work, and I knew that he knew.)

I nodded. There wasn't any use trying to explain that I had forgotten it was in the bunch of valentines I'd "mailed" that morning, and that I hadn't really decided for *sure* that I intended to mail it.

I wondered how he'd gotten it.

"It's a good thing I always go through the valentines before we pass them out," he said. "I try to intercept the ones that might hurt people."

Silence. I could hear the clock ticking.

"You don't really want to give this to Ruby, do you?" he asked.

I shook my head. Already it seemed like the worst idea I'd ever had. I couldn't imagine why I'd even considered it.

He handed it back to me. I tore it in half, and then again, and in smaller and smaller pieces before dropping them in the wastebasket.

I wanted out of that room. Fast. I was ashamed, embarrassed, heartsick that Mr. Van had seen such a mean and ugly side of me. He wouldn't want to read any more of my poetry now. He probably couldn't stand the sight of me.

Maybe not, but he wasn't through yet. He motioned me back to my seat and did a little arranging and stacking of the papers on his desk while he seemed to be thinking of what to say next. At last he looked at me.

"You have a gift for writing, Emily," he said. "Don't misuse it. Do you understand what I mean?"

I did! I did! I would never, ever write

poison-pen things about Ruby or anybody else. Even if they were true.

Then Mr. Van was his kind, pleasant self again. "You may go now, Emily," he said. "And I expect the next poem you let me read will be one you can be proud of."

He smiled at me, and the sun came out again.

I went home to write some proud-making poetry, but first I gave myself a penance: I was going to have to make a really *nice* valentine for Ruby.

Chapter Seventeen

MARCH CAME, and Norman won the city marbles championship. We were all happy for him. He even got his picture in the paper and he carried the clipping around with him until it got all soft and ragged. It did wonders for his grumpy disposition too.

In our little world, things were going along pretty much as usual, but something terrible was going on in Europe. The dread word *war* hung over us all like a black cloud. We started having something called current events every morning at school, and Mr. Van would pull down the big map and point out the faraway places where the trouble spots were. Every day there were more of them.

One day I opened a magazine and saw a painting of a schoolhouse not much different from Park School, with crowds of children running out the door and looking up in terror at the airplanes flying over and dropping bombs all over the place. The children's eyes were wide with fear and their mouths were round *O*'s of screaming.

Probably I wasn't the only kid making bargains with God, selfish bargains like "I'll never complain again because Daddy won't let me wear snow pants if You won't let the war come over here."

I asked Mama why God let wars happen. She just stared out the window, sighed, and said that some things didn't seem to have an answer. But my job, she said, was just to go to school and do the best work I could.

But I knew that many nights she lay awake a long time thinking about the poor homeless, hungry children in Poland and Czechoslovakia, and then felt guilty because she was so glad that her own children were all well fed, warm, and safe under our own roof.

Well, safe for the moment, anyway. I think we all felt that our little world, our country, our city, our very homes were not the secure, solid, invincible fortresses we had thought them to be.

Ruby alone didn't seem much affected by events in the outside world. She lived in the here and now.

"There's going to be a May Festival," she

whispered. Her little brown eyes sparkled with excitement. "With a maypole and a May Queen and everything."

What was a May Festival? What was a maypole? I wasn't about to ask Ruby. I knew I didn't have to. She would tell me.

"How do you know?" I asked.

"Oh, I heard it somewhere," she said vaguely.

Eavesdropping again. Probably outside the teachers' lounge, with her ear glued to the door.

Well, I didn't know what Ruby was getting so excited about. If there was going to be a May Festival and a May Queen, it wasn't likely to be *Ruby* wearing the crown.

I thought *I* had a pretty good chance. After all, I had gotten the most valentines on Valentine's Day. (And Bobby *did* send me one, but he didn't sign it "Love." He signed it "Like.") And Mr. Van didn't send us valentines, but he gave us all little cellophane packages of heart-shaped "red hots." I planned to save mine forever and ever, but Buddy and Joe-Joe found them and ate them. They said they didn't, but their lips and tongues were dyed red.

I had all A's on my report card too, so didn't I seem like a likely candidate for May Queen?

I tried the title on for size. Her Royal Highness Emily Ann Campbell. Not bad.

Maybe *this* was going to be the way I left my mark on Park School? Somehow it was a kind of letdown. Disappointing. There just wasn't anything very *significant* about being May Queen of Park School. It was an honor, of course, but a kind of, well, *frivolous* honor, if there was such a thing. Not quite in the same class as, say, little six-year-old Mozart being invited to play the harpsichord for Marie Antoinette.

I carried the news home after school.

"I'm probably going to need a new dress," I announced.

"Oh? Why is that?" Mama asked.

"There's going to be a May Festival," I explained, "and a May Queen."

"And you've been chosen the Queen of May?"

"Well, not exactly," I said. "At least, not yet."

Mama looked at me thoughtfully for a long time.

"I don't think I'll start on that dress just yet," she said. "Let's wait and see."

I went off to The Barn to sketch a May Queen's dress that would be the envy of Princess Elizabeth and Princess Margaret Rose.

Several days went by and we didn't hear anything at school about the May Festival. Maybe there wasn't going to be one after all.

"Oh, yes, there is," Ruby insisted. "Wait and see."

She was drawing something in her tablet and coloring it with her crayons. When she saw me looking at it, she turned the page over and began copying arithmetic problems from the blackboard.

But she wasn't quick enough. I had seen her picture. It looked a lot like my sketch of a May Queen's dress.

Was Ruby drawing a dress for *me*?

I didn't think so.

Several more days passed by (with Ruby and me both covering page after page in our tablets with secret May Queen dress sketches) before we got the official news. It came from the music teacher.

Miss Renoe comes to our room once a week to teach us singing and give us something called music appreciation. She brings along with her a small portable record player and a stack of phonograph records. She plays Beethoven and Mozart and Haydn, and the difference between the music that Miss Renoe plays and the kind of music that Violet Rose's sister Mildred plays is even greater than the difference between some poets I could mention. Although, since I have started writing poetry of my own, I know how hard it is sometimes to make what you *write* sound as good as what you *want* to say, and I am not as critical of Mr. Longfellow as I used to be. I believe the poem that Mr. Longfellow had in his *mind* when he wrote *Paul Revere's Ride* was probably a really good poem!

We had just finished listening to Rossini's *William Tell Overture* (familiar to us, only we called it the "Lone Ranger's Song"). It was a rousing favorite of ours. Miss Renoe always had us tap out the rhythm on our desks with our pencils—a dangerous practice. She had to relearn every week that once we start tapping, we don't want to stop. It goes on in little echoing spurts long after the music stops.

"Boys and girls! Boys and girls!" she trumpeted above the staccato pencil beating. "I have an important announcement to make."

When the last pencil gave a final feeble beat and she had our attention, she continued.

"This year Park School is going to hold a May Festival, sponsored by the P.T.A., and the sixth grade has been asked to sing."

She didn't get any further. At the words "May Festival," Ruby's hand shot up.

"Is there going to be a May Queen?"

"Yes. Yes, there is," Miss Renoe admitted.

"Who is it?" Ruby persisted.

"Why, why, it's *you!*" sputtered Miss Renoe who couldn't seem to think fast enough to dodge Ruby's questions. "A committee of parents and teachers made all the plans."

Ruby settled back in her seat with a satisfied look.

Well, I was astonished. *Ruby* the May Queen? How could that be? I don't suppose the fact that Ruby's mother is president of the P.T.A. had anything to do with Ruby being chosen queen? Maybe yes. Maybe no.

Then I happened to glance up at one of the many mottoes framed in a row above the blackboard. WIN OR LOSE, BE A GOOD SPORT, and I knew I had lost and it was good-sport time.

"Congratulations, Queen Ruby," I said.

I won't say I wasn't surprised.

I won't say I wasn't disappointed.

But there were two good things about losing, I decided later. First, now I didn't have to worry that I was going to leave my mark on Park School in that trivial way, and second, Mama wasn't going to have to make me a new dress.

Chapter Eighteen

I HAD TO HAVE A NEW DRESS after all. Ruby chose me as one of her two ladies-in-waiting. Fern (the girl who called her mother "Della") was the other one.

Our job, as far as I could tell, was to do everything Ruby told us to do.

"Wear a blue dress."

"Curl your hair."

"Walk two steps behind me."

"Smile a lot."

"Keep your eyes on me."

"Stand up straight."

Fern was happy just to be part of the May Festival. She didn't seem to mind having Ruby boss her around.

I minded. I minded a lot. But I would rather be boiled in oil than have Ruby know it. I kept a smile on my face by pretending that Ruby was really Queen Marie Antoinette and that any minute the Revolution would start and she would be carted off to the guillotine.

It's not that I especially wanted to be a May Queen. It's just that if there was going to *be* a queen, I wanted it to be me! Is that so bad?

Ruby held rehearsals every day at recess out under the tree at the edge of the school yard. About half the kids in school, mostly girls and little kids, stood around in a circle and watched. Ruby tried to shoo them away, but she didn't seem to have much royal power.

"This isn't *your* school yard, Ruby!" they said.

"You're not a *real* queen!"

About then Mr. Van rode up on his white horse (this is a figure of speech!) and rescued us just in time to prevent a full-scale riot. He suggested that if we kept on holding a May Festival rehearsal every recess, everybody would be so tired of the whole idea that nobody would come to the real thing. Even Ruby could see the wisdom of that, and we all went back to playing Run, Sheep, Run and Capture the Flag.

At home, Mama was busy sewing my new dress. We had picked out the material together, a soft, thin blue and white cotton print that looked like a summer sky with wispy bits of white clouds drifting across it.

I stood on a chair while Mama marked where the hem would go.

"Stand still!" Mama said, her mouth full of pins.

I kept twisting around, trying to see my reflection in the dresser mirror behind me. I liked what I could see. Mama had designed the dress herself. She never needs to buy a pattern. She just takes her tape measure and runs it around me in a couple of places, makes a few pencil marks on a newspaper, cuts out her own pattern, and stitches away.

The top part fit just right, easy and roomy. I could raise my arms, bend and stretch, and not feel anything tight and binding. When it comes to clothes, comfort still comes first with me. But I don't mind if they're pretty too.

This dress was pretty. There was a line of tiny white buttons marching down the front, and delicate white-lace edging around the neck and around the loose cuffs of the puffed sleeves. What I liked best of all was the full gathered skirt that draped in a thousand tiny folds to my knees. I gave an experimental twirl, knocked a few pins out of Mama's mouth, and almost fell off the chair.

"Emily, *could* you stand still just for a

minute?" Mama asked patiently.

For once, I didn't envy Ruby and her closetful of store-bought dresses. She couldn't possibly buy one as pretty as this. I even told Mama so.

I told Ruby too. Well, she asked for it.

"I guess your mother is making your dress," she said.

"Yes," I said, "and it's the prettiest dress in the whole world."

Ruby didn't even hear me. "Mine came from St. Louis," she said. "From Stix, Baer and Fuller. My mother and I took the train and spent all day shopping. It's awfully hard to find clothes that fit when you're as tiny as I am."

"Yes, that's too bad," I agreed sympathetically. "It must be awful being so little."

That wasn't at all the reaction Ruby was looking for and I knew it, but I was getting really tired of hearing about Ruby and her "I could fit into a cigar box" size.

We were all hoping for good weather, since the May Festival was going to be outside behind the schoolhouse. The janitor had set up rows of wooden folding chairs for the audience and built a low stage where the "royalty" would sit. He had rigged up a lighting system for stage footlights with yards and yards of extension cords. He'd taken the chained bar swings off the "turning pole" and it was going to be strung with long, different-colored paper streamers. Twelve little fifth graders were practicing a kind of weaving dance they'd do, holding the streamers, that was supposed to wrap the maypole from top to bottom in a pretty colored pattern of ribbons, if they did it right.

Miss Renoe was drilling us in "Welcome, Sweet Springtime," and a couple of other songs about spring, in case anybody missed the point.

The weather forecast was good, the fifth graders had finally gotten so they could dance around the maypole without getting all tangled up, and Ruby, Fern, and I had practiced how to walk slowly down the aisle between the rows of wooden chairs, with our heads held high and not giggling or waving to our friends and relatives in the audience. It looked as if this May Festival would go off without a hitch. Until two days before the event.

It wasn't my fault that Ruby didn't get to be May Queen. In fact, I even felt sorry for her. I know what it feels like not to be May Queen, and it must be a thousand times worse if you have the crown snatched right out of your grasp at the last possible moment.

It's not much fun having mumps either, which is what Ruby got.

She didn't even get to be the first one to wear her tiny new dress from Stix, Baer and Fuller. Her mother brought it to school in a big flat dress box, and it was kind of like Cinderella and the glass slipper as she looked over the sixth grade to see if there was anyone small enough to wear it.

"There has to be a queen," she said, "and it isn't likely that anybody here has a dress pretty enough."

It's easy to see where Ruby gets her famous tactless way of speaking. But Mrs. Weber meant well. Maybe Ruby does too. Sometimes.

Mrs. Weber took the lid off the dress box, folded back the layers of tissue paper, and carefully lifted out the May Queen's dress.

It was pale sunshine yellow, with a gauzy full skirt and lots of little skirts under it. It looked so light and puffy that you almost expected it to rise up in the air and float away like a balloon.

And just as in the fairy tale, our own little sixth-grade Cinderella, Violet Rose, was the only one who could wear it. She looked like a princess too.

"Maybe my sister Mildred could sing and play her guitar in the program," she said hopefully.

"Oh, I don't think so, honey," Miss Renoe said. "We've got everything all scheduled and the program is all printed. Maybe another time."

The night of the performance, everybody who was in the program was supposed to come a little early so we could get our last-minute instructions. I put on my new blue dress proudly. Maybe it wasn't as fancy as the Stix, Baer and Fuller May Queen's dress, but it was a very pretty dress anyhow, and a lady-in-waiting isn't supposed to be fancier than the queen, is she?

As I peeked around the corner of the building, I could see some of the audience had already arrived. Violet Rose's family had all showed up to see her be the May Queen. What with all her brothers and sisters, they took up the whole first row. And right on the aisle seat, dressed in her cowboy boots and hat, was her singing sister, Mildred. She was holding her guitar. Just in case.

Chapter Nineteen

MY RED-BEARDED GRANDPA, the one who tells ghost stories, was visiting us again. He thinks he has special powers. He says on a good day he can see into the future, and sometimes he can even make things happen just by thinking about them.

"Then make the sun shine tomorrow," said Mama. "I plan to do the laundry."

"You don't believe me," sulked Grandpa. "It's a terrible thing when your own daughter doesn't believe in you."

"Oh, I believe in *you*, all right," said Mama. "But I don't believe you or anybody else is magic and I wish you'd quit filling the children's heads with nonsense."

Mama needn't worry about me. I liked Grandpa's stories but I never believed them. I don't believe in ghosts and magic, myself. I even have a hard time with Joan of Arc and her "visions" and "voices," though it's in all the history books.

Still, some days you just wake up with a kind of mystical feeling that something wonderful is about to happen. Today was one of those days.

"Is *this* it?" I thought as I sat down to one of Mama's special breakfasts of apple pancakes. I ate three, but the look-out-for-something-wonderful feeling was still with me.

On the way to school I saw a little pocket of violets in a mossy spot under a cottonwood tree, and I stopped to watch two cardinals building a nest, and I felt the soft spring breeze blowing around my bare legs now that winter was over and I didn't have to wear the ugly long stockings.

Even if nothing else really great happened today, it ought to be enough just to be alive on this bright, shiny May morning, I thought. But the miracle feeling was still there. I felt like our old coffee pot when the water begins to boil, about to *percolate* with sheer joy and delight and well-being. I couldn't walk. My feet broke into running and skipping without any regard for the fact that I'm almost twelve years old.

At school, the morning wore on much as usual. Mr. Van was his ordinary wonderful self, looking like a fairy-tale hero, how I imagined Sir Galahad would look in a brown wool suit.

Then I reversed my daydream and pictured Mr. Van in a Sir Galahad outfit—armor, visor, gauntlets, shield, the whole works. He was dazzling.

It's a sad thing to fall in love when you're only eleven years old and don't have any choices. You have to live the life that other people arrange for you.

The school year would be over soon. Before me stretched a bleak future. This time next year I'd be in a different school, a different world, a world with no Mr. Van in it.

If I thought my grandpa, the magic one, could really change the course of events, I'd ask him to keep me in sixth grade forever. I know. That's not the right answer. There isn't any answer. I just hope that when I am older, I'll fall in love with somebody else. But right now I doubt it.

With all these gloomy thoughts in my head, I was beginning to wonder about my early morning conviction that something wonderful was going to happen today. Apparently Grandpa's mystical ability to see into the future—even the *near* future—had not been passed on to me.

It was reading time, everybody's favorite time of day. Mr. Van had finished *Robin Hood* long ago. It had been followed by *Tales of Paul Bunyan*, and *Robinson Crusoe*. Now we were halfway through *Treasure Island* and we lived in delicious suspense from day to day as Jim Hawkins went from one narrow escape to another.

But what's this? Mr. Van wasn't reaching for *Treasure Island*.

He was holding a letter in his hand.

He cleared his throat.

"Class! Let me have your attention. One of our sixth graders has received an award that brings a great deal of honor to Park School."

We all looked around the room at each other. What could it be? Who could it be? Had Norman won a *national* marbles championship? Was Lance going to play his violin with a symphony orchestra? Had Ruby been named tap-dancing champion of the western world?

It wasn't any of them.

It was me.

"Without her knowledge," Mr. Van confessed, "I submitted one of Emily Ann's poems to the National Grade School Poetry Contest, and her poem will be printed in a book of the best fifty poems submitted."

I was at a loss for words.

Ruby wasn't. "Did she win a prize?" she wanted to know.

Mr. Van smiled. "She got an honorable mention."

"Too bad," said Ruby, looking across the aisle at me. "Too bad you didn't win a prize."

"*Too bad?*" Mr. Van frowned. "I don't think you understand, Ruby. There were over one thousand entries from schools all over the United States. Only fifty poems were chosen to be printed in a book. There was a first place, a second place, and three honorable mentions. Just being selected for publication is an honor, and to be among the top five in one thousand entries is a very great honor."

"Oh," said Ruby.

Then everybody clapped. Even Ruby. Even Mr. Van.

I still felt dazed, but I was curious too. I'd written a lot of poems for Mr. Van during the year. I wondered which one had been chosen.

Mr. Van glanced at a piece of paper on his desk. "I don't believe the class has heard your poem 'God in April,' Emily Ann. Would you read it to us?"

"I don't have a copy with me," I said, "but I think I know it by heart."

I walked slowly to the front of the room, trying to get the lines straight in my head. My heart was beating a little faster than usual. It wasn't exactly stage fright. I *liked* being there, but it's not quite the same thing as sitting in your seat and listening to somebody else being "it."

I looked out at the classroom full of faces turned to me, waited a moment until they were quiet and until *I* was ready, then I began:

God in April
by Emily Ann Campbell

If I were God in April
I'd never do a thing
But wander down a country lane
And hear a bluebird sing.

I'd drink from every babbling brook,
I'd run down every hill;
I'd pick a blue-eyed violet
And a yellow daffodil.

I'd dance with all the butterflies,
I'd fly with all the kites;
I'd laugh through all the shining days
And dream through starlit nights.

I'd go barefoot in dewy grass,
I'd sing a happy song.

*If I were God, I'm sure I'd
Make it April all year long!*

The class clapped, and I went back to my seat. Mr. Van smiled, thanked me, picked up the copy of *Treasure Island*, and pretty soon we were all sitting on the edges of our seats, hardly daring to breathe as Jim Hawkins matched wits with Long John Silver. Everybody except me, that is.

Someday I will have to read *Treasure Island* all over again. There are whole pages that I heard with my ears that day, but that didn't make a dent in my consciousness. My mind was busy thinking about poetry! *My* poetry! Printed in a book! Honorable mention!

I wanted to run straight home and tell Mama about it.

Mr. Van kept me after school again.

"This is for you," he said, handing me a certificate that said, in fancy Old English printing, that Emily Ann Campbell had been awarded honorable mention in the National Grade School Poetry Contest for the year (of Our Lord) 1938–39.

"They sent two copies. I thought I'd frame the other one and put it in the trophy cabinet in the front hall," Mr. Van said, "if you don't mind."

Mind? Mind? Why should I mind? Maybe it wasn't as great as those historical markers all over New England proclaiming that "George Washington Slept Here," but as a way of leaving my mark on Park School, it would do.

I knew right away where I was going to put *my* copy of the award. On the wall of my writing room in The Barn. Maybe in the years to come the whole barn wall would be papered with awards! And maybe not just honorable mentions. Second prizes. First prizes. Maybe I'd even get *paid* for writing! Who knows?

"And here's something else," Mr. Van said.

He handed me a slim notebook with a blue cover. There was a white label on the front that said:

The Original Poetry of
Emily Ann Campbell
Park School
1938-39

Inside were all my poems, neatly typed and very professional looking.

"I made two copies, one for you and I'd like to keep the other. Just in case you get famous some day. Maybe you'd autograph it for me."

I could tell he was half teasing. Maybe three quarters teasing. Maybe even 100 percent teasing, but I didn't care. I took the fat black Schaefer fountain pen he held out to me and wrote my name with a flourish inside the cover of his copy.

And as I wrote, I had a sure and certain feeling that I would be doing this same thing over and over again in the years to come, in other places, with other books. Maybe it was a little bit like Grandpa and his magic. I could see into the future! . . . at least, I could look at the past and guess and *hope* what the future might be. And while there didn't seem to be any Mr. Van in my future, there were many other exciting and wonderful things about to happen, and one of them was going to be writing. Lots and lots of writing.

I told Mr. Van, "I will always remember that you were the one who got my very first autographed book!"

"Many happy returns," said Mr. Van, just as if it was a birthday. Maybe it was. The birth of Emily Ann Campbell, Writer.